A FAE'S FATE

The Complete Story

ABIGAIL GRANT

FANTASY & PARANORMAL ROMANCE

Copyright 2022 ©
Abigail Grant

This is a work of fiction. Names, characters, places and incidents, either are products of the author's imagination or are used fictitiously.

DEDICATION

Thank you to my incredibly supportive husband for believing in me and taking our three little hooligans away long enough for me to write to my heart's content!

Thank you to my family and friends that always ask how the writing is going or tell me you miss me when I've been stuck to a computer for far too long.

And an extra big thanks to those readers that tell me when I drop the ball or when I blow you away. I never imagined making it this far, and I wouldn't be here without you!

CONTENTS

PART 1: A FAE'S FATE	18
CHAPTER 1	20
CHAPTER 2	24
CHAPTER 3	28
CHAPTER 4	36
CHAPTER 5	42
CHAPTER 6	46
CHAPTER 7	50
CHAPTER 8	56
CHAPTER 9	60
CHAPTER 10	66
CHAPTER 11	72
PART 2: A FAE BORN	76
CHAPTER 12	78
CHAPTER 13	84
CHAPTER 14	90
CHAPTER 15	94

CHAPTER 16	100
CHAPTER 17	106
CHAPTER 18	112
CHAPTER 19	116
PART 3: A FAE'S BLOOD	124
CHAPTER 20	126
CHAPTER 21	132
CHAPTER 22	138
CHAPTER 23	142
CHAPTER 24	148
CHAPTER 25	152
CHAPTER 26	156
CHAPTER 27	162
CHAPTER 28	168
PART 4: A FAE TORN	172
CHAPTER 29	174
CHAPTER 30	178
CHAPTER 31	183
CHAPTER 32	188
CHAPTER 33	194

CHAPTER 34	200
CHAPTER 35	206
CHAPTER 36	210
CHAPTER 37	214
PART 5: A FAE CROWNED	218
CHAPTER 38	220
CHAPTER 39	224
CHAPTER 40	230
CHAPTER 41	236
CHAPTER 42	242
CHAPTER 43	246
CHAPTER 44	250
CHAPTER 45	254
CHAPTER 46	258
CHAPTER 47	262
REVIEW THIS BOOK	266
OTHER BOOKS BY ABIGAIL	267

PART 1

A FAE'S FATE

CHAPTER 1

NERA
12 Years Old

"Nera, cover up before we get to the fairgrounds." My brother Benjamin flicks the tip of the pointed ear that pokes out one side of my hair.

I slow my speed-walking as I hurry to fluff up my brown waves so they disguise my ears. "Better?" I ask, turning from side to side for him.

Benjamin grins down at me from his nearly six-foot height. "The ears are covered, but how do you suppose we get rid of that nose?"

I gasp and cover my nose as Ma reaches back from where she walks ahead of us with Pa. She smacks my brother on the arm. "Benjamin Lewis Larc! There is nothing wrong with your little sister's nose!" She turns to me with a gentle smile. "You have a perfect little button nose, my dear. Don't let your freckle-face brother tease you."

I snort and nearly trip over my boots as Benjamin's jaw drops. "Pa, your wife just made fun of my freckles!"

He pokes our father in the back, but Pa is already laughing right along with us girls.

Pa turns to give me a loving wink, the corner of his eyes scrunching up in that way that I love, and then he raises his thick brown eyebrows at Benjamin. "My *wife* is your mother, and if you can't take a little teasing from the woman who gave you life, don't dish it out."

Benjamin scoffs and throws one of his large arms around my dainty shoulders. "Come on. I love my little Nera Deera. What kind of brother would I be if I didn't give her shit now and again?" *Ugh, I hate that nickname.*

"Language!" Ma shouts, making Benjamin and I both flinch. When Ma means business, she can be scary, and she is *not* okay with foul language, even if Benjamin is nearly a man at fifteen-years-old.

I check my ears once again, being sure that they're covered before we step onto the dirt of the bustling fairgrounds. All kinds of people move about the large area, setting up tents or playing games. A clown on stilts taller than Pa walks past us, and I have to squint to look up at him. He gives me a wink and then steps right over my head, making me giggle with delight.

This is my favorite time of the year, just before the weather grows cold and we're stuck at home through winter. It's also one of the only places I'm allowed to visit since Ma and Pa have me studying from home all year long. I inhale the scent of cotton candy and bonfires, wishing I could bottle the smell and take it home with me.

A permanent smile is etched into my face as I practically hop beside my family as we take in the sites of the traveling fair. There are so many people here that it's almost overwhelming, but it's also incredibly exciting.

"Oh, I want to see the magician!" Benjamin shouts, pointing toward a stage set up beneath a wall of oak trees. The sign reads "REAL MAGIC" and my heart pounds with excitement.

"You know it's not real, son. They're just tricks," Pa says, steering us away from the stage.

Benjamin throws his hands in the air. "How do you know it's not real? Everyone knows that magic exists."

"But not in the Mortal Lands," I add, knowing that magic doesn't ever come across the Night Woods barrier. At least, that's what I've been taught.

Ma nods. "Nera is right. Magic isn't allowed around humans. We are simple here, with easy and safe lives. I prefer it that way."

"How do you know a few of the faeries or elves haven't snuck onto our lands? I mean, just look at Nera." Benjamin points at me, causing my cheeks to heat with a blush.

Our father snaps his head around and shushes Benjamin harshly. "Quiet about that, son! There are many people around us, so that talk will not be allowed."

Benjamin grimaces and his eyes cast down to the dirt at his feet. "I'm sorry, Pa. I wasn't thinking."

I touch Benjamin's arm, letting him know that I'm not upset with what he said. If I had it my way, I'd let the humans of our large village know all about me. I've never wanted to hide, but Ma has made it clear throughout my life that nobody can know about my…*differences.*

"They won't understand," she has said. *"People can't see beyond what they know."*

So, I hide my pointed ears and I keep up with my daily meditations. I can't let my emotions show, or my eyes will change color, and that's definitely not something that humans can do. I keep out of the public schools, and I don't go to parties or sleepovers. Basically, I live a dull life. But I trust my parents and I know they only want to protect me.

"Who wants some kettle corn?" Pa asks, lightening the mood.

"Me!" Benjamin and I say together and laugh.

Pa buys us the biggest bag of kettle corn that the booth has, which ends up being half of my height. I've stuffed my face so full that I could explode, when my eyes land on a sparkling purple sign above a black tent.

"FORTUNE TELLER"

I sit up straight, my heart fluttering with hope as I grab Ma's hand. "Ma, I know you've said no in the past, but I'm older now." I plead with her with my big blue eyes that she says make her melt.

"What?" She asks hesitantly, her brown eyes looking around for what I could possibly be asking for. She spots the black tent and her shoulders sag. "Nera, I'm not so sure that's a good idea."

I bat my eyelashes at her and stick my lower lip out. "Come on. I'm twelve! I know that these people can be hacks and liars, so you know I'll go in there with low expectations. Just please let me have the experience. That's all it is, just some fun."

Ma looks toward the boys who both just shrug back at her, no help at all. Then she sighs and I immediately know I've won. "Fine. But, if I say we leave, then we leave."

"Of course!" I nearly shout, gripping her hand in mine. "Let's go!"

I drag my mother behind me and head straight for the fortune teller tent. It's about time I find out why I came to this human world. Why I was left in the Night Woods as a baby for my parents to find and adopt. *Who am I, and where do I come from?* Only one way to find out.

CHAPTER 2

NERA
12 Years Old

There's no line in front of the fortune teller's tent, so I slip right through the black curtain and into the dark room. Ma's hand squeezes mine as she trails hesitantly behind me, but she's letting me finally look for the answers I've wanted my whole life. I can't possibly turn back.

Purple twinkle lights drape around the inside of the tent, illuminating the space in an eerie glow. An older woman with smooth gray curls sits at a small, circular table in the center, her eyes sparkly green as they look me up and down.

Her red lips rise at the corners into a knowing smirk as she gestures to the empty bench in front of her. "Welcome, ladies, to my humble fortress. Please, take a seat and tell Madame Karista what you seek this evening."

I move around the metal bench and settle down, pulling Ma down beside me. "Hello, Madame Karista. My name is Nera." I give her a wobbly smile. "Shouldn't you already know what it is that I seek, since you are psychic?"

The woman throws her head back with a laugh, clapping her hands together with a jingle from her many bracelets. "Oh, I just love when the spunky girls come to visit. Yes, Nera, I am very aware of why you're here. I was only curious as to what it is you wish to learn from me first. You have many questions in that sweet little head of yours, do you not?"

I nod slowly, still unsure whether Karista is the real deal or not. "Yes, Madame. My whole life, I've wondered who I am and where I come from. I hope you can tell me what you know."

Ma clears her throat beside me, drawing my eyes up to her. "I already know who you are, Nera. You don't need this woman to give you those answers. You're my daughter–"

I hold up my hand, stopping her explanation. "Ma, it's not that I don't appreciate the life you've given me, but you and I both know there's more to me than what you see. Please let me figure it out."

Ma nods just as Madame Karista leans on her elbows and grins at me. "Yes, Nera. You are something that the humans around you may never fully understand. Even if the Fae saw you, they would be unable to comprehend the extent of your power."

I swallow hard, my eyes going wide. I blink rapidly, forcing my irises to remain blue and not give away the sudden fear that trickles through my body. "Wh–why would the Fae care about me?"

Karista raises a thin eyebrow at me. "Are you not a Fae child, Nera Larc? I know you attempt to hide it, but I see it, clear as crystal."

"We should go, dear," Ma says, tugging on my arm.

I shake my head. "Not yet, please." I turn back to Karista. "Do you know who it was that abandoned me as a baby?"

Karista shakes her head. "I can only see the moment you began to cry in your bundle of blankets, and your Pa running out into the Night Woods to take you home. He was brave to enter the woods that night."

I smile softly. "He says he couldn't ignore the sounds of my cries. He felt like it was his own child calling out to him."

"You *are* our child." Ma squeezes my hand tightly, her eyes wet with unshed tears.

Madame Karista reaches across her table and grips my free hand. "You are incredibly lucky to have the home and family that you have now, and although I can't tell you where you came from, I can let you leave with a warning." Her green eyes sparkle brighter as wrinkles deepen around her cheeks and she focuses on something within me. "You do not have an easy road ahead. Somebody knows about the secrets you try desperately to hide, and they will be after you. You're not safe in your home, so leave *now*, before it's too late."

"Nera, don't listen to this," Ma says angrily, dragging me to my feet.

I fight her grip and stand before the fortune teller. "What do you mean leave now? Leave to where? What about my family?"

Karista keeps her heavy gaze on me. "Your human family has no place in your journey, Nera. Your absence can only help them."

"Stop!" Ma yells, but Karista keeps talking.

"Keep your emotions hidden, for only you to see. Protect your magic, and your heart, but also know that your heart will not be solely yours forever. There are so many trials ahead of you, but you were born to survive, and you are more than what eyes are able to see. Trust in your gut every step of the way, and accept help from the unexpected."

Karista stops talking and her face softens as she looks up at me. Her words swirl around in a jumbled mess inside of my mind. It makes no sense. I want to ask her more, but

Ma drags me out of the tent and back to Pa and Benjamin before I can begin to process the woman's words.

"Never again, Nera," Ma says, taking my face in her hands. I look up into my mother's loving eyes as she repeats her words to me. "We're never doing that again; do you hear me?"

I nod, my body suddenly becoming too cold out in this late summer heat. All I can think about is Madame Karista's warning playing on repeat in my mind.

"You're not safe in your home, so leave now, before it's too late."

CHAPTER 3

NERA
12 Years Old

I stretch out on my back, staring up at the different colors draped above my head. After meeting the fortune teller, Ma was quick to get us all back to our home at the edge of the Night Woods. This is the only home I've ever known, and it's comforting to be here, lying beside Benjamin in our makeshift fort of blankets and pillows.

Benjamin has always known just how to cheer me up when I'm down. The attic is our special place, where we can talk away from our parents about anything and everything. My hair is thrown up in a bun at the top of my head, letting my pointed ears breathe freely. I don't need to hide here.

"What are you thinking about over there, Nera Deera?" Benjamin sits against a mountain of pillows, his sketchbook in hand as usual.

I sigh and roll onto my side, dragging my knees to my chest. "Do you think magic is truly real, Ben? That the City of Shifters, and Elf Mountain really exist beyond the Night Woods?"

He shrugs, setting his pen and book to the side. "I don't know for sure, but I like to believe the stories are true."

"Even though these creatures could be dangerous and hold power over us?"

Benjamin scoffs. "Humans can be dangerous too, Nera. Humans murder and rob one another, so why would I be afraid of magical creatures that could do the very same things?" He raises his eyes to the blankets above us. "I mean, isn't it incredible to imagine a person that could shift into an animal? Or, even a dragon?" His eyes widen in excitement. "Where's the fun in life without believing in the impossible?"

I smile at his awed expression. "You're right. It is enchanting to think of another world beyond our simple life. It sure can get boring here."

Benjamin sticks his foot out, nudging me. "What about what that fortune teller lady told you? Do you think you're really in danger?"

I sit up, shrugging my shoulders. "I mean, I hope I'm not in danger here…"

"But?" Ben asks, raising an eyebrow at me. He knows me so well.

I roll my eyes. "But…when she spoke of my future, like I could really have some adventure. Like I have this power inside of me that actually means something. That gave me hope I guess."

He nods. "You don't want to be trapped in this house forever. I get that."

I grin back at my big brother. "You're lucky that you're going to art school in the city. It's going to be so much fun."

He chuckles warmly, a sound I know so well. "Come on, Nera Deera. Aren't you going to miss me even a little?"

I shrug as if the thought of Benjamin moving far away doesn't break my heart. "I won't miss the teasing, or the smell of your feet after a long day of working on the farm with Pa."

Benjamin growls at me, diving forward to tickle my waist. "You're such a little pest!"

"Stop, Ben! I give up!" I cry out between laughter, kicking at Benjamin's large body.

Just when I'm ready to scream from the torture, a loud banging sound rings out through the house, causing Benjamin and I both to freeze.

"What was that?" I ask, whispering for some reason.

Benjamin sits up straight, his head tilted to the side while he listens. Muffled voices come from outside the house, followed by more banging against wood. Someone is knocking on our door.

"It's the middle of the night," I say. "Who would be–"

Benjamin holds a finger to his lips, shushing me. He stands and pulls down a few blankets, revealing the large attic around us. He tiptoes over to the small attic window and peers outside. I can hear more shouts, louder than before, but I can't make out what the voices are saying.

An orange glow lights up the dark night outside the window, and then more pounding on wood vibrates through our home. "Benjamin," Pa's voice calls up the stairs of our home. "Get her out, now!"

I stare wide-eyed at my brother as he moves quickly away from the window and to my side. "Get up, Nera. We need to go." He drags me to my feet by my elbow and runs over to my slippers that are discarded by the attic door. Benjamin tosses the slippers to me and then digs through some old boxes. "Put those on."

I stick my bare feet into the soft slippers that rise just above my ankles. "What's happening, Ben?"

He's digging through box after box. He drags one of Pa's old sweaters out of one box and pulls it over his head before tossing me another one, then he drags out a dull pocket knife and sticks it in his pajama pocket.

"Ben!" I shout, trying to get him to answer me as I follow his lead and put the oversized sweater on over my head.

My brother turns on me, his eyes hard and focused, a look I've never seen on his playful, carefree face before. He looks like a man, not a boy anymore. "I'm taking you into the Night Woods, Nera. We're going to climb out the window and down the back of the house."

"But..." I have questions, but I hear the front door of the house fly open and slam against a wall, followed by many voices yelling and the sound of a shotgun going off.

My whole body is shaking in fear as Benjamin once again grabs me and tugs me across the floor. He unlatches the round window and pushes it outward, over the roof ledge that juts out the back of the house. Benjamin climbs through first, ignoring the battle going on below us. He turns and waves for me to follow him with his finger to his lips again.

I don't need him to tell me to shut up. Fear has already stolen my voice away from me. The house shakes from movement downstairs, and I hurry after Benjamin. We both crouch on the roof ledge together, scooting along the slate shingles toward the tall trellis that Pa built for Ma four summers ago.

Benjamin leans over the top of the trellis, scanning left and right before he lays flat on his belly and pushes himself backwards over the edge. He's quick and precise in his movements, like he's done this a hundred times before.

"Come," he whispers to me, helping me follow him onto the trellis.

I find my footing in the open parts of the wood and climb beside Benjamin to the bottom. Before my feet even hit the grass, Ben is tugged from behind and pulled onto his back. I gasp as a man that I've seen a few times in town tackles my brother and kicks him in the side.

"Ben!" I call out, dropping the last few feet to the ground.

Benjamin rolls to the side and pushes himself to his feet. The man charges after him again, but Ben is quick as he pulls the pocketknife out of his pocket and flicks it open. "Get back," he says, danger in his usually kind eyes.

The man tries to swat the knife away, but Benjamin is fast. He slices the blade across the guy's arm, drawing blood. Then, not even seconds after, Benjamin sticks the knife into the man's chest, dropping him to the ground.

I throw my hands over my mouth in shock as I look up at Benjamin who is already moving toward me. My brother just stabbed someone, and he barely blinked. He looks around one more time, the night surrounded by the sounds of shouting and screaming.

"Where is she?" A deep voice calls out from within the house.

I look up at Benjamin again. "Ben?"

He shakes his head, and without a word, he grips my hand and pulls me across our yard toward the line of trees that border the Night Woods. I've never been into the woods before. It's forbidden to enter the Night Woods unless you're a registered hunter. But, even the best hunters don't always come home alive.

Our feet cross into the pitch black of the woods, and I stick my slipper heels into the dirt, barely stopping Benjamin. "Ben, please tell me what's happening." He tries to tug me again, but I drop to my butt. "I'm not going in there until you talk to me!"

He whirls on me, dropping to his knees and whisper-shouting. "Nera, don't let them hear you!"

"Who?" I ask, tears forming in my eyes. "Who is after me?"

Benjamin looks back toward our home which is lit from the inside, and then his eyes fall on me with sadness. "Ma and Pa told me years ago that if anyone in the village found out about what you are, they would consider you dangerous." He pauses. "They would want to see you killed, Nera."

I blink up at him, shaking my head. "But, I've kept hidden. Nobody knows." I look back to the body lying in the grass. "That man was after me?"

Benjamin nods. "Yes, Nera. Pa has been training me to fight for a while now. He said that if the village turns on us, I would need to get you out and take you into the woods. Tonight, that happened."

I get back on my feet. "But, our parents! We have to go back and help them."

Benjamin grips my upper arms tightly. "Nera, I'm doing my job as your brother by getting you out. Pa wanted it this way. Please, let me help you!"

A sob escapes me as I look past Benjamin's shoulder toward the house once more. My eyes fly open wide when I spot the two men running toward us, one of them with a pistol pointed right at Benjamin's back.

"Ben, move!" I scream, shoving him out of the gun's sight.

He barely shifts to the left as he follows my gaze. The piercing sound of a gun going off cracks through the air, and as if in slow motion, the bullet flies toward my brother and strikes him in the shoulder.

Blood splatters my face, and Benjamin falls forward, almost knocking me down with him. He cries out in pain, his hand going to his shoulder. "Nera, run! Now!"

I look down at him and then back to the men gaining distance, almost to the woods now. "I can't leave you, Ben! I can't!"

Benjamin's eyes plead to me as he holds his bleeding arm. "If they get another shot, it will be at you. Run now, and do not come back." His eyes are now wet with tears, matching my own. "I love you, baby sister. Remember what the psychic said. You can't stay here. Go find your destiny, okay?"

"I love you, Ben." I nod slowly, knowing it's now or never, and I spin on my heels before running as fast as I can into the dark Night Woods.

I block out all sound around me, and I run until I can't run anymore. *Go find your destiny, okay?* I will.

CHAPTER 4

NERA
12 Years Old

I can't run anymore. I can't.
    My legs are tired, my lungs burn, and my eyelids are heavy. I've slept twice already since I left Benjamin. I have no way to tell the time in these woods. The sun never shines, leaving me in an eternal night, but I know at least one day has passed. I've traveled for miles, running, walking, dragging myself forward. The Night Woods have to end eventually…hopefully.
    The rustling of leaves and breaking of twigs around me are the only things keeping me going at this point. I'm afraid that if I stay still for too long, something will find me. The legends of these woods play on repeat in my mind. Sprites that peel the skin off of bodies. Fae animals with razor-sharp teeth and an insatiable hunger. Shifters on the hunt for lost prey. *I'm lost prey.*
    At some point in the past mile, I have stumbled into a sudden winter. Flurries of snow fall all around me, and I can feel the cold seeping into my bones. At least I know I'm not traveling in circles, but even that can't comfort me.

I've lost my family. I don't even know if they're alive at this point. I left my father and mother fighting for their home, and my brother bleeding from a gunshot wound. And now I'm going to die from hunger and exhaustion, maybe freeze to death. I can't help but wonder if I deserve this end after abandoning my family.

I drop to my knees, my legs finally giving out once again. I roll onto my back and tug my father's sweater tighter around my body. It smells like him. Like sandalwood and home. I blink, feeling a new round of tears coming on, but no wetness comes. I'm too dehydrated to cry now.

"Is this the end?" I ask the woods. "I'll never become a woman. I'll never find my destiny." My dry throat causes my voice to crack as I talk to the darkness around me.

I wiggle my freezing toes, my feet poking through the bottom of my slippers now. A sharp laugh escapes me at the state I'm in. Torn and stained pajama bottoms. An oversized jacket covering my small body. My hair is strewn around my face now, pointlessly covering my ears like it always has.

"I'm a faerie, you know?" I blink up at the dark canopy of trees, listening as snow crunches in the dark. Something is out there. Maybe it will kill me fast.

"Will you kill me quickly, forest creature? I don't have a lot of meat on my bones."

I can't even lift my head off the soft pillow of snow beneath me. Maybe if I close my eyes, I won't feel the pain. My heart pounds, but my mind can't comprehend the fear of this moment as footsteps come closer to me. A low growl floats toward me from the dark, making me shiver even harder.

"Please make it fast," I whisper, my eyelids heavy as they try to flutter closed. "Please."

Sleep drags me under, but not before a flash of golden scales and shining golden eyes moves above me. A tightness wraps around my waist, and then I'm floating into a perfect cocoon of sleep.

My eyes flutter open, and I'm greeted with an orange glow of light surrounding me. Snow falls in the distance, but my body is coated in such a warmth that the cold can't reach me.

Last thing I remember, I was lying on the forest floor, freezing to death while something hunted me from the dark. *Is this heaven?*

I try to turn, to rise from where I'm lying against stone, but a voice hushes me and a hand runs through my tangled hair. "Rest," the voice says in a whisper.

I'm immediately struck with a new fear, and I struggle against whoever it is beside me. It's not Benjamin, nor is it my parents. I don't know this voice, but I don't have the strength to fight it either.

I try to speak, but it sounds more like a whimper, and the hand passes through my hair again, lulling me back to sleep. "Just rest now."

A cold wind is whipping at my skin, waking me from a nightmare. I dreamt of Ma, Pa, and Ben. They were crying out for me, pain etching their voices. I'm not home, though.

I blink against the harsh wind, and a sharp gasp leaves my mouth when I spot the tops of green trees flying past me from below. My body launches into fight mode and I kick the air, my throat too dry for the scream that wants to come.

Something growls above me, causing me to crane my neck back to see what made the sound. My blood runs cold at the sight of a large, golden dragon soaring through the early morning sky, holding me tight within its talons.

I look down at my waist where the dragon holds me tightly, my father's tattered sweater filling with cold air. How did I get here?

I wonder where the person went that kept me warm and safe. I pry through my mind for any memory of the voice that calmed me while I slept, but I never saw the person.

"Put…" I struggle to speak past my aching throat. "Put me…down," I rasp out, hoping the beast can understand me.

The creature peers down at me through golden eyes, studying me for a long moment before looking ahead again. We fly like that for a few more minutes before the woods come to an end, and a large city of buildings spans across a wide valley.

My jaw drops as I take in the cobbled streets that weave between homes and shops, still sleeping before the sun rises, all leading to tall, snow-covered mountains that hug an incredible castle within their canyon.

The dragon quickly descends toward the ground at the edge of the long forest, which I'm guessing is still the Night Woods. The long, golden wings of the beast beat rapidly as we approach the street beside a large manor home.

The dragon veers toward the manor, dropping me gently on the front porch of the home before landing its massive body just a few feet away. I try to push myself to my feet, but I stumble back, my head hitting the front door painfully.

The dragon's head turns from side to side as it studies me with those piercing gold eyes.

"Where am I?" I ask the beast. "Why did you bring me here?"

I know it can understand me, but it doesn't make a move to respond. I open my mouth to speak again, but the dragon quickly huffs out a loud snort and then launches itself back into the lightening sky and disappears beyond the trees.

I sink back onto the cold stone porch, my body exhausted and spent from the past few days, or maybe weeks. I don't know anymore. I can hear voices from within the manor behind me, but I can't even knock on the door.

I just want to sleep, so that's what I do. I sleep.

CHAPTER 5

REINOR
7 Years Later

I bend backwards, the deadly blade flying so close to my chest that a button slices off the front of my shirt. Wide-eyed, I stand up straight and look at my long-time friend in his cocky, blue eyes.

I look down at my ruined shirt and back at Elex. "I truly don't understand why the king took so long to bring you on."

Elex chuckles, twisting his sword in front of him for show. "Yes, that king can be a strict one. I feel sorry for his children." He raises an eyebrow in my direction, humor in his tone. "For four years I've applied to be a trainer, but hey, I'm here now."

"And I wouldn't be the swordsman I am now without your guidance, Elex. We should have been celebrating your success four years ago."

He shakes his head. "Nah, you were rotten with a blade back then. All limbs and no muscle."

I take a step forward and slap my friend on the arm. "I was also barely eighteen. I've grown, and I can kick your ass now."

"Well, your dragon can kick my ass, your highness. The man with a blade, not so much." Elex grins, and I hate that I know he's right.

I groan, refusing to give an answer to him. I sheath my sword and sit back on the grassy hillside behind the rear castle walls. This is the spot I go to escape, and Elex and I can talk freely.

Elex Minara is the best swordsman in the entire City of Shifters. He has been training me since we were both young boys, him just a year older than myself. Today is the day that he has officially been named the royal swordmaster. He deserves the title, and I wish I could have given it to him years ago.

Elex's father was the chosen blacksmith for *my* father, King Iredras, as well as his army. Elex's father passed away just a year ago, and now my friend is making it on his own, a fierce wolf shifter in the army, and now swordmaster. I'm proud of the one person in this city that calls me their friend, instead of their prince.

As the dragon prince of shifters, my life has been luxury, pampering, everything the shifters in the city consider a dream, but they don't see it all. My father rules harshly, and he has raised his children in the same way. We are beneath him, insignificant until the day he dies and it's our turn to be just like him.

The only love I have ever felt is from my mother who died when I was too young to appreciate her scent or the sound of her laugh, leaving my younger brother, Calder and myself without a gentle hand to shape us.

Calder is ruthless, the exact replica of our father, and I would likely be the same…if it weren't for *her*. Seven years ago, I laid eyes on someone that clung to my heart and refused to let go. At that time, she was no more than a child, weak and lost. I stumbled upon her in the Night

Woods the same day my mother left this world. I was running away from my grief, letting my dragon take control so I didn't have to feel.

I couldn't leave the girl behind. She would have died there in the cold if I ignored the pull I had toward her. The only reason I ever came home was for her, and even though I can't stand my life as Prince Reinor Iredras, I can never regret that day.

"I know that look, Reinor." Elex pulls me from my thoughts. "I know what day it is." He eyes me with his arms crossed over his chest. "You're going to ditch me, aren't you?"

I look down at the old leather watch on my wrist, and my heart races as I take in the time. "I'm sorry, man. You know I can't miss it." I'm already on my feet, stripping out of my torn shirt and tossing my sheathed sword to Elex.

He accepts my blade and clicks his tongue. "I wouldn't dream of holding you back. Plus, everytime you see her, you're a lot nicer to me. You practically float around the castle like a happy little faerie."

I roll my eyes as he flutters his hands at his sides like he's flying. "The Fae are anything but happy floating creatures. You ever even met one?"

He waves a hand at me. "Psh. I don't need to. They have frail wings and sparkling eyes. If that doesn't say 'sweet and pretty', then I don't know what does." He flexes his muscles. "Now, wolf shifters. We're terrifying, quick and wild."

I scoff. "If wolves are terrifying, what are dragons?"

Elex rubs his pale chin, pretending to think on my question in the most dramatic way possible. "Aha! Dragons are…delicate." His grin makes me growl as I call upon my shift.

My dragon emerges in moments, my heavy, clawed feet slamming against the green grass beneath me. I flare my dragon wings out to the sides and huff out hot steam down at my now-tiny friend.

He looks up at me with a heavy roll of his eyes. "Fine, you're not delicate, just a fool in love."

If I could tell him he's wrong, I would. But, as I launch my heavy body into the darkening sky, I know he speaks the truth. It wasn't love at first, when I was a broken teenager, and she was just a lost girl. Over the years, we both grew up, and now thoughts of her eclipse everything else. I *am* a fool in love, and I can't stop myself from making the same mistake every single month.

CHAPTER 6

NERA

I hurry and shove as much fruit as I can into my waiting basket, knocking a metal spoon off the kitchen counter in the process. *Dammit!* The spoon clangs against the stone floor before I can catch it, and I freeze in place, listening.

Nobody comes running into the kitchen, so I let out a breath of relief. I grab a long baguette and add it to the basket with the rest of the stolen food. I guess, it's not technically stolen if I live here, right? *Wrong.*

I may sleep in that small closet in the basement of this extravagant manor, but I am not one of them. I am a servant, nothing better than a rat. Well, a rat that can cook and clean for them, and be their ball when they need to bat at something.

For seven years, I have lived under the roof of this family of shifters at the edge of a grand city. Since the morning I was dropped on their doorstep. The moment Mrs. Cragore, the panther shifter, welcomed my cold body into her home, I felt safe. I felt cared for as I cried in her arms and her husband ordered their maid to help me bathe and set me up in a comfortable room for the night.

They introduced me to their daughter, Teyla, who was just a year older than me. We became instant friends, and I couldn't believe my luck to be left to such a loving family when I couldn't have my own.

Their love lasted until a day later, when they discovered my pointed ears and realized I was Fae. Apparently, in the City of Shifters, the Fae are nearly as welcome as they are in my human village. Mr. Cragore told me I should be cast out and left for dead, but he would keep me around as long as I could serve him. *For free, of course.*

I've done my job, been kept fed and alive, and that's the only reason I'm still here. Well, that and for Teyla. Without her, I would have left years ago.

"Nera, hurry up in there," Teyla whispers to me through the kitchen door.

I jump at her voice, and then quickly settle, grabbing one more hunk of elk jerky before running to my friend's side. "I'm done. This should be enough."

Teyla and I hurry out the back door of the kitchen that leads to the empty courtyard behind the manor. She grabs my hand before I can escape through the black iron gate. "You need to stop doing this, Nera. One of these days, you will get caught."

I look into her beautiful, dark gray eyes. She truly is a vision with her tan skin, high cheekbones and sleek frame. She's a panther shifter, yes, but even in her human form she is very much the gorgeous feline.

I take her hand in my free one. "Tey, he is the only thing that gives me hope. Can't you see that?"

Teyla nods as she squeezes my hand. "I'll talk to Mom again in the morning. You're nineteen now and I'll be moving on when Mathis finally proposes. I know I can convince her to let you leave with me."

I sigh. Teyla is like a sister to me, but she will never understand the life I live just two stories beneath her. I work until my hands bleed, while she attends schooling in the city. I am beaten when I can't complete my chores on time, while she goes out on dates with her loving boyfriend, Mathis.

Once a month, I take what food I can and run off into the Night Woods with true excitement and joy in my heart. It's the only thing I look forward to in my day, and I can't fully express that to Teyla. I told her just a few years ago about where I sneak off to each month, and she has kept my secret like the loyal friend she is, but she worries about me.

I wrap Teyla into a hug. "Even if they don't let me leave with you, Tey, I'll get out of here. You are the only reason I stay."

"I know that, and I hate it too. I'm going to make something of myself, okay? And I will share that life with my sister one way or another." She winks at me, making me grin.

"Oh, I have no doubts." I kiss her cheek quickly before escaping through the gate.

In five steps, I'm into the Night Woods, and just another small hike into the dark and I will see *him*. Every second Sunday of the month, right at sunset, he meets me here, since that first night that I stumbled upon him when I ran out here to hide.

He promised me that day that he will always be here, and he has never broken that promise. My mysterious stranger, the boy of the Night Woods, the boy who stole my heart.

The day that my village came to my home to kill me, I lost everything. I lost my parents, and I lost my brother. I've wondered for years if they're still alive, and if they ever came looking for me. I'd love to sit under a blanket fort with Benjamin and tell him of the magic I've seen in this world.

People shift into animals around me regularly. Real magical beings exist beyond the human world we knew, and Benjamin would love it. If only I could share it all with him, but I can never go back. I wouldn't survive the Night Woods a second time.

39

CHAPTER 7

REINOR

The green tops of the Night Woods span out all around me, like an ocean that never ends, but I know exactly where I'm going. I turn my dragon head from side to side, making sure nobody can see me across the city, and I drop down into the trees, leaving the glow of the setting sun behind, and entering the dark.

These woods are eternally night, making travel through them difficult and often deadly. Thanks to my dragon sight, I can see well in the dark. I land heavily, my large talons digging into the dirt beneath me. I call back my dragon and quickly locate the tree that has been my hiding spot for years.

With one reach up into the twisted branches, I drag out the backpack that I placed here when I was seventeen. I hurry and dress in a simple pair of long pants and a tattered black tunic. I stick my feet into the worn leather boots that have seen better days. It's just another lie. I may be Reinor Iredras, the dragon prince, but not in these woods.

Here, I'm just Reinor, the human traveler that calls the Night Woods his home. I'm simple, dressed in average clothes and without access to magic. It's how she sees me, and in all honesty, I prefer this person over the golden prince.

I shove the backpack into its hiding place and run eagerly to our usual meeting spot, my heart already racing in anticipation.

I round a tall boulder and stop in my tracks at the beautiful creature waiting for me. Her long, dark hair hangs in waves around her pink cheeks. She's shorter than female shifters. Of course, she's not a shifter at all. She hides from me behind her silky hair, but I've seen her pointed ears.

"Nera," I breathe out her name, causing those bright blue eyes to capture me. Her eyes shift slightly to a red color before she takes a heavy breath and they return to blue.

I wish I knew what the color of her eyes meant, but I can't ask her. She thinks I'm merely a human, and she has told me that she is a panther shifter. I can't tell her that I know the truth. That I know she is Fae.

Nera sighs and her lips lift into a welcoming smile when she spots me. "Reinor, you're here." She says my name the same way every month. Like she can't believe I came for her.

I laugh and tilt my head. "When have I not shown up for you, huh?"

Nera shrugs, hoisting the basket in her arms a little higher in front of her thin waist. "You're here every month, at the same time and place. I guess I feel like eventually you'll get bored and move on."

If only she knew how addicted I was to her. "How could I leave when I know I'll get to see you each time?" I take a step forward and point to her basket. "I have told you to stop bringing me food. I'm fine without it."

She shakes her head as usual. She's stubborn. "You live in the Night Woods, all alone. I don't know how you do it, but if I can make it any easier, I will continue to do so."

I smile down at her and snag the basket from her arms. "Come, eat with me." I sit with my back against a thick tree trunk, watching as Nera takes the spot just across from me. The ground here is worn from the many years we've sat in this same place together.

I open the basket and find a plethora of food within, which causes my heart to sink. What does it take for her to feed me like this? Do her hosts allow her to take their food or is she forced to steal it? I have more food than I could ever ask for up at the castle, and servants to cook for me each day. I don't deserve this, and Nera doesn't deserve the lies.

"Stop making that face, Reinor," Nera says with strength in her voice.

I look up at her, and I know she can see the guilt in my eyes. "What face are you referring to? I don't make a face."

She rolls her blue eyes and shoves my folded leg with her foot. "The face that says 'I am too chivalrous to take food from a girl'" She mocks my voice by lowering her own, sounding ridiculous.

I chuckle and run a hand through my brown shaggy hair. "It's as if you know me, Nera."

Her eyes soften and I'm frozen as she trails her gaze down my body and back up. I don't know if she meant for me to see her perusal, but I liked it. *A lot.* "I do know you, Reinor. I may not know your day-to-day life, where you grew up, or even your last name, but I know that you are loyal, kind, funny, and honest."

I flinch slightly at the last word. *Honest, I wish.* I try to hide my shame with a smile as I take a big bite of the bread she brought me. "You seem to think quite highly of me. I'm not sure I'm so deserving."

Nera shrugs again, never one to dive too deep into conversation. "Eh, you're alright, I guess."

I scoff, and she laughs along with me. Her laughter has a way of seeping into me in the most comforting way. I could fall asleep to that sound every night of my life.

I watch Nera tear off her own hunk of bread and eat with me. I didn't always have these feelings for her. The day I found Nera lost in the woods, covered in snow and so broken that she was close to death, all I knew was that she was a young girl in need of help. She looked as lost as I felt.

The day my mother died, I wanted to die right along with her. I was fifteen, and had no idea how to live my life without her in it. It was my father's words that made me run away from home. *"You will be the dragon king one day. Dragon kings do not retreat within themselves just because of grief."*

I didn't want the responsibility. I didn't want to be a dragon king if it meant I was unallowed to mourn my mother openly. I learned to control my dragon shift the summer before, so I knew I could get away. I shifted, and I left into the Night Woods, hoping to find a new version of myself there. Instead, I found Nera.

I lifted her from the snow during a blizzard and took her to a cave just outside of the City of Shifters where I built a fire and cared for her until I was sure she was past the worst of it. I remember her trying to speak to me in the cave, and I was so afraid that she would run from me because Fae and shifters aren't friends.

That fear was the reason I chose to leave her outside of a random home. Someone I hoped would care for the lost Fae girl. I returned home after that, back to my royal life. My father never even knew that I left.

For two years, I checked in on Nera each month after that first day, watching from a distance, hoping to catch a glimpse of her on the grounds of that home. She looked healthy, and I felt okay knowing that I had done at least one good thing with my life.

Nera was fourteen the Sunday that I sat at the edge of the woods to do one of my usual checks. When she burst through the back door of the manor and ran barefoot into the Night Woods, I couldn't stop myself from going after her.

I followed her for nearly a mile into the trees, and that's when she spun and her sad, purple eyes locked onto mine. Her cheeks were stained with tears and every part of me wanted to run to her and hold her until the pain went away. She blinked away her tears, her eyes returning to their usual blue before she asked who I was and why I followed her.

That's where the lies began.

"Reinor." Nera's voice interrupts my thoughts. I look up at her and she shifts uncomfortably. "Do you ever wonder what the other lands are like? I mean, I figure you know the Mortal Lands well since you're from there, but what about Elf Mountain, or the Fae Wilds?"

I clear my throat. "Not really. I like it here...why wonder when I know I'll never leave?"

Her eyes fall to her hands, her shoulders sagging. "When I met you, I was still a kid. I'm a woman now."

Trust me, I know.

"And, now that you're a woman, you want to leave?"

She looks up at me again. "I want to be free, Reinor. Like you."

If only she knew how wrong she was. I shake my head. "I'm not free." It's barely a whisper, but she hears it.

Nera leans forward, sitting on her feet as she looks me directly in my eyes. "You are more free than anyone I've ever known. How can you say you're not?"

I groan, moving the basket from between us. I want to grab her and tug her onto my lap. I want to tell her all of my truths, to make her see the real me and accept that man. I want so much that I can't have.

My hands itch to reach out to her, but I leave them on my thighs. "You're right. Still, you can't just run off like me. This is no life for a girl like you, Nera." I can't help but grab one of her hands in mine, and that touch alone warms my chest. "Remember the day I found you crying?"

She nods. "Of course I remember that day."

"You told me you were crying because you didn't know where you belonged. After you returned home and we decided to meet like this each month, you have been happy. You have a good life...don't you?"

I stare into those beautiful eyes, her hand in mine, and I wait for her to tell me she's happy...but she doesn't.

CHAPTER 8

NERA

Happy? I must be an incredible liar if Reinor believes me to be happy with the life I live. The only time I'm truly happy is when I'm here with him.

I try to keep my breath steady as I focus on the weight and warmth of his rough hand gripping onto mine. His fingers rub along my knuckles so slowly that goosebumps rise along my arm. We have always joked, talked about everything, but nothing of real consequence. But, in all the time we've spent here in this spot, Reinor has never touched me like this.

"Aren't you, Nera? Aren't you happy?" His golden-brown eyes bore into mine, begging to know my answer.

I bite on my bottom lip, knowing that I should lie, but I've lied for so long now. Maybe I can actually tell the truth for once. "No, Reinor. I'm not happy at that house."

Reinor leans back like he was just struck by my words. Since day one, Reinor has known that I'm just a ward in the house I live in. I never went into details about my real family, but I told him that I was orphaned at a young age and my host family has been incredible to raise me as one of their own. *Gosh, what a lie that was.*

Soft fingers grip onto my chin as Reinor raises my face to look him in the eye. He's so close to me, just a foot away. "Nera, has your host family not been treating you right? What's going on?"

I lick my lips. I can't tell him everything. "It doesn't matter. I'm not happy, and I want the freedom you have." *Just be brave, Nera. For once, do something for you.*

My hands shake as I lay my palms on Reinor's thighs and scoot myself between his outstretched legs. He drops his hands and his eyes widen slightly as I move closer to him. I don't know how to do this, how to touch someone. My heart beats in my ears as I settle myself just inches from the man I can't stop thinking about.

"Nera," Reinor rasps my name out. He swallows hard, his golden eyes locking onto my lips. "Wh–what are you doing?"

"I think I'm being bold," I say, daring myself not to run. I reach a shaking hand up to his shaggy brown hair, letting my fingertips dip into the soft locks that I've dreamt of touching for years before drawing back again.

Reinor's eyes flutter before connecting to mine, and I swear the gold glows brighter in his irises. "Let me help you," he says with a small lift of his lips.

His large hands cover mine where they rest on his thighs, and he slowly strokes his fingers up my arms and over my shoulders. One of his hands slips behind my neck, beneath my hair, and his other cups my cheek oh so gently. He's too good at this, likely experienced.

"I've never kissed someone before, Reinor. I–I don't think I know how. You might not like it."

Reinor smiles sweetly with a warm chuckle as he licks his lips. "You already know way more than you think, Nera. I haven't even tasted you yet, and I'm hooked."

He doesn't wait for me to back out. His grip on the back of my neck tightens and he pulls my lips to his. *Oh, wow.* Reinor's mouth isn't just warm, it's hot. His lips slide against mine so slowly, letting me adjust to this heady sensation. I match his movements with my own, exploring the different angles that our lips can fit together, and my hands begin to take on a life of their own.

I slide my palms up Reinor's chest, amazed at how hard his body is under my touch, and I press up on my knees so I'm leaning over him. He moves his hands down my back, and in one swift movement, he grips my backside and lifts me off the ground to settle me onto his lap, my legs straddling his.

A gasp leaves me, causing our lips to break apart, and Reinor groans in disappointment. I smile at his reaction and hurry to press my lips to his again. My arms snake around his neck and his wrap tightly around my waist, squeezing me against his hard body so that not an inch separates us.

I've never felt so complete, and so safe in my entire life. A small whimper escapes me as soon as Reinor's tongue strokes against my eager lips. I want this always, this intoxicating feeling, his arms protecting me, his mouth claiming me. *I want Reinor.*

I break our kiss to catch a much-needed breath and I know my eyes have changed colors, but I hope he isn't frightened by the magic. His shining eyes peer back at me and his hot breath fans my face as we smile back at one another.

"Take me with you," I whisper, knowing that this is what I want for my future.

His entire body freezes, even his breath as he leans back to study my face. "What do you mean, Nera?"

I place my hands on his chest and hope he can feel what I feel. "Take me away from here, Reinor. We can live freely together, out there in the woods. I won't ever have to go back to that house."

His eyebrows furrow as he watches me and the lips I just kissed dip into a frown. He seems to think on my words, but his head shakes subtly from side to side. "Nera, we can't…"

My heart sinks, cracking into pieces as it falls to the dirt. I grab his arms and take them off of my waist, giving myself room to crawl backwards off of his lap. He lets me retreat, and that hurts just as much as his words.

I get to my feet and take a few steps away from Reinor, trying to catch my breath. I whirl on him as he stands too. "What do you mean we can't? Why not?"

"Because, we just…dammit, we just can't, okay?" He barks the words out. His lips tighten together into a thin line. His face is unreadable, and unwelcoming. This isn't the Reinor I've come to know.

I watch him for a long minute, hoping he'll give me something more. "You kissed me, Reinor. Didn't—" I hiccup, my emotions boiling to the surface. "Did that not mean anything to you?"

Reinor's face softens and he steps toward me, but I take another step back. "Of course it meant something, Nera. It meant *everything*."

"But not enough to be with me?" I blink back the tears that threaten to pour, fighting to keep whatever dignity I may still have.

He stares at me, his smooth jaw clenching tightly, his fists closing and opening at his sides. Why is this so hard for him? He closes his eyes tightly, and when he finally speaks again, I know this is over.

"Go home, Nera. It's getting late."

I smooth my hands down the front of my old dress, trying hard to not break down, fighting to swallow the hard lump in my throat. "Bye, Reinor."

I turn to leave when his voice makes me stop. "Will you come back next month? Promise me you'll be here."

I hesitate. "I will," I tell him, and I run off without even a glance back. *No, I won't be back next month. I won't see Reinor ever again.*

CHAPTER 9

NERA

How could I be so stupid? How could I believe for even a second that he wanted me? I shake my head and wipe the remainder of my tears away before quietly sneaking through the back kitchen door. I expect to be greeted with darkness, but a light switches on as I enter.

I gasp and take a step back, only to freeze when I catch the sneer on Mrs. Cragore's face. She is the lady of the house, which means the kitchen is a disgusting place to her. *"A room for the help, not a civilized woman."* So, why is she here?

"Madam," I dip my head to her, wiping once more at my puffy eyes.

She takes a step toward me, her lavish skirts swaying with her walk. "And where exactly have you been, *faerie*?" She spits out the word *"faerie"*, as if it tastes rotten on her tongue.

I keep my head low as I speak, remembering the times I tried to stand tall to this woman and quickly regretted that choice. "I'm not sure what you mean, Madam. I have been here, tending to the garden all evening."

Mrs. Cragore scoffs. "I have been looking for you for the past hour. I checked the garden, the washroom, the basement, and the kitchen. Now, well past dark, you come barreling in like you've just run a mile." She grips my chin roughly, forcing me to look into her gray eyes where she stands inches taller than myself. She is beautiful, so much like her daughter, but with an ugly heart. "Now, tell me the truth!"

I grind my teeth together, wishing I could fight back, but her panther form is ten times stronger than my small body. "I went for a walk…in the Night Woods."

I don't have time to even flinch as the back of her hand strikes my cheek so hard that I stumble to the side. It takes another few seconds for the pain to register, and it aches all the way to my skull, causing new tears to fill my eyes.

"Those woods are forbidden!" Mrs. Cragore screeches at me in her high voice. "Go to your room this instant, you wretched *beast*, and do not leave until you are summoned!"

I find my footing once more and rush through the kitchen toward the servant entrance, where I take two stairs at a time down to my basement bedroom. I quietly shut my door and fall to the floor, drawing my knees to my chest where I let the sobs pour from my body.

I don't cry from the pain of being slapped. I've experienced much worse at the hands of the Cragore's. I cry for the loss of the most important thing in my world. My only safe haven in this life that was forced upon me. *Reinor.*

I don't know how long I sit on my floor in sorrow, but a soft knock brings me to my feet. "Nera, I'm coming in."

I sigh, relieved at the sweet sound of Teyla's voice. She steps quietly into my bedroom, knowing that if she were caught down here, we'd both be punished. Her with words, me with fists. Teyla takes me in, her eyes trailing from my likely blood-shot eyes to my swollen cheek. I haven't seen the result of her mother's slap, but from the grimace on Tey's face, it doesn't look well.

"Oh, Nera. I'm so sorry." She steps up to me and pulls me into her pajama-clad arms. "How did Mother know you were gone?"

I shake my head. "She needed me for something, who-knows-what. When she saw me sneaking into the kitchen, I guess she knew I'd left the grounds. I told her I went into the Night Woods."

Teyla hisses. She knows the repercussions of entering those woods. "Will she report you to the castle guard?"

I shrug. A part of me hopes Mrs. Cragore won't report me to the guard for entering the woods. The punishment is imprisonment and starvation for a time. Another part of me feels like it would be a relief to be anywhere but here.

"Let's not worry about that now. We shall know by morning, I guess." I settle onto my bed and pull my friend down beside me. "Did you see Mathis tonight? Has he finally proposed?"

Teyla blushes. Mathis Longborn is the city's most eligible bachelor, and panther shifter. He has been courting Teyla for months now. I don't believe she loves him in the slightest, but she's happy for the match since he is a relatively kind man, and can support her for the rest of her life. Teyla wants to be free of her parents every bit as much as I do.

"We sat at the park and talked for a while. He kissed me on the cheek before we said goodbye, and I felt absolutely nothing." Teyla sighs with a groan and falls back on my bed. "At least he is nice to me. Who needs passion, right?"

The memory of Reinor's lips claiming mine floods my mind, and I hurry to turn away from Teyla. That kiss was certainly passionate, but it clearly meant more to me than it did to him. Maybe I'd rather have Teyla's tame, no butterflies relationship.

"Something is going on with you, Nera." Teyla sits up and tilts her head in front of me. "Talk to me."

I rub a hand over my face, flinching when I touch the bruise on my cheek. "Something happened between me and Reinor, and I don't know how to feel about it."

I look into Teyla's gray eyes and pour my heart out to her, giving her every detail of my night out in the woods with Reinor. I tell her of the kiss, of his reaction to me asking to run away with him. Of the way he made my heart soar, and also break within minutes of each other.

By the time I've finished talking, Teyla is wiping away a tear of her own. "So, are you going to run away, then? Is that what you've decided?"

I chew on the inside of my cheek. "I'm not sure, Tey. I can't stay here, and I can't follow you into your impending marriage. I need to find myself, but the City of Shifters doesn't want me."

"I want you," she says sadly. "You're my sister."

"And I will love you forever, no matter where I end up." I pull her into a tight hug, and then we say our goodnights.

I am wrenched from sleep with a force that turns my stomach upside down. Large hands grip my arms in a painful way, and I am suddenly brought into the moment and out of my peaceful dream.

"Wha–" I start to ask what's happening, until I realize that Mr. Cragore has a tight hold of me, and is dragging me from my bedroom.

"Shut your mouth and walk, beast!" He growls at me, his eyes flashing silver like his panther's.

I find my footing and stumble after him through the basement and up the stairs, until he shoves me out the back door of the house and onto the lawn. It's early morning with a cold dew that has settled on the grass. I try to stand, but Mr. Cragore sticks his boot into my back and shoves me back down onto the wet ground.

I turn my head toward the man that has called me his servant for years. Behind him, two large men that I recognize as shifters on the manor's security detail stand with their arms crossed behind their backs. They stare on as Mr. Cragore leans over me with a sneer.

"Why are you doing this?" I ask him, my arms and back aching now.

His eyes narrow on me as he points a long, thin finger my way. "I was kind to you the day you appeared on my doorstep, *faerie*. I gave you shelter and allowed you a position on my staff. And you repay me and my family by stealing from our kitchens!" His voice turns shrill with his accusation.

I flinch under his venomous anger. "I didn't steal anything!" It's a lie, but I can't tell him the truth.

Mr. Cragore growls low, his eyes flashing silver and his nails growing into sharp claws. "You are a thief and a liar! I should have banished you to the Night Woods years ago." He turns toward his guards. "Men, grab the girl. We are taking her to the castle."

"No," I gasp out.

My face pales, and the blood running through my veins turns to ice. I know it's Monday, and every Monday is the day of trial. The king sits in his courtyard to hear the complaints of his people, which often ends in at least one public execution. If Mr. Cragore drops me at the dragon king's feet, accusing me of thievery, I will surely die today.

The two large guards each grab one of my arms and hoist me to my bare feet. I pull against their holds, but it's useless. I'm small and weak, without any shifter strength. "Please, let me go! I didn't do anything wrong!"

I look into the eyes of the men, but neither of them will listen to me. They're employed by the Cragores. They need to continue to get paid, and they owe me nothing.

"Nera!" Teyla's voice calls out to me, and I twist my neck around to see her running from the front of the house in her pajamas. She steps in front of me and shoves at one of the men. "Let her go, now!"

The guard doesn't budge. I look into my friend's eyes. "Tey, stop. It's no use." Tears are stinging at my eyes, and I can see her own fill with wetness.

"Teyla! Get back into the house!" Her father grabs her arm and tugs her away from me.

"No," Tey screams, fighting her father. She looks up at him. "Where are they taking her, dad?"

"She is to be tried at the castle for her crimes."

Teyla gasps and covers her trembling lips. "Dad, no! You can't let them kill her!"

"She is a thief," Mr. Cragore snaps. "It is time to say goodbye."

Teyla turns to me with tears dripping from her cheeks. "Nera, you can fight them. You have to!" She sniffles and tries to reach me, but her father pulls her back to his chest. "You're stronger than you think, okay? Don't stop fighting."

I nod to my dear friend. "I promise." I don't know how I'll fight this day, but I can do it for her. "I love you, Tey."

"I love you too," she whispers. Another man that I hadn't noticed grabs Teyla around the waist and carries her back toward the house. "No, no, no!" She screams and fights against the guard as he takes her farther away from me.

"Now, let us go to trial," Mr. Cragore says, straightening his suit jacket before leading the way up the cobblestone street.

My two guards drag me along and I do all that I can to stifle my tears. I won't cry for these people, and I will not die today.

CHAPTER 10

REINOR

When I've heard the term "heartbreak" in the past, I never could have imagined a heart could feel this sort of pain. Watching Nera run from me last night was the most painful thing I've ever felt. She said she'll return and meet me again next month, but I knew it was a lie. I hurt her by telling her we couldn't run away together, even though all I wanted was to say yes.

Honestly, I've dreamed of what it could be like to kiss Nera, to hold her in my arms the way a man should hold the woman he loves. Having her lips move against my own, and her delicate hands touching me, I wanted to give her the entire world. But how can I do that when she doesn't truly know me? I'm nothing but a lie to her.

"Dammit!" I sit roughly on the edge of my bed, throwing my head into my hands. I pull at my hair, wanting nothing more than to rip the strands from my scalp. Anything to replace the ache in my heart, and the vision of Nera's back running away.

My bedroom door swings open, slamming against the wall behind it. I jump up, ready to fight, but I scoff when I see my little brother, Calder. "What the hell are you doing, Calder?"

He rolls his eyes, similar to my golden-brown ones, and he folds his arms over his barrel chest. "Father left for Elf Mountain this morning. Did you know of this?"

I shake my head. "No, he doesn't exactly tell me about his comings and goings."

Calder steps close to me and drops a hand onto my shoulder. "Well, Thomin informed me that my elder brother will be holding our father's place in the kingdom until he returns in two weeks!"

My whole body stills, and I can't stop the clench in my jaw. "So, I'm expected to be the king for two weeks?" I rub a hand over my unshaved face. "That's just great." *Sarcasm, so much sarcasm.*

Calder shrugs and a cocky grin stretches across his face. "And I somehow knew this before you. Why they insist on you running this kingdom over me is ludicrous." He slaps my arm hard. "Good luck, brother. You are *so* going to need it."

He laughs evilly before turning back toward the hall. He stops just outside my door before turning back toward me. "Oh, right. It's the day of trial. Your highness is expected in the courtyard immediately." He winks and saunters away.

I groan, closing my eyes tightly for a few seconds, reminding myself to breathe. Calder is trouble, always has been. He takes after our father too much for me to fully respect him. If he were to be the heir to the shifter throne, I would fear for all shifter-kind. Alas, the role falls to me, even though I loathe the idea of ruling.

I know why Thomin, our father's right hand, didn't warn me of my latest responsibility. I didn't come home until early this morning, choosing to fly over the city under the moon until my wings ached. If I had been home last night, I could have been better prepared.

I shake the thought away and leave my bedroom to make my appearance in the courtyard. I hate this day. The day of trial. My father considers it necessary for a weekly trial for the citizens to air their grievances in front of their ruler. Someone is almost always executed this very day, and I can't stand the pettiness of it all.

I make my way through the castle doors, and I cringe at the sound of angry shouts that float across the castle courtyard. People are here, ready to complain to me, and I don't have the heart for it.

I steady myself and try to put on a strong front as I take the final steps to the throne waiting for me in the courtyard. A crowd has gathered, but I don't want to look at their faces. They delight in the punishments of others, and though they are my people, they don't have my respect.

I hear shouts of "thief", "outsider", and one shout that has me freezing in place. "Faerie!"

I spin toward the line of citizens waiting to present their complaints, and the entire world stills as my gaze locks onto an achingly familiar pair of eyes. She isn't looking at me. She is hunched over, barely being held up by two men at her sides. Her feet are bloodied and bare, her blue eyes cast down to the ground, and her long black hair hanging loose over one shoulder, revealing one of her pointed ears for all to see.

Nera.

I swallow the hot anger that has boiled into my throat, and my fists clench tightly at my sides. Nera, *my Nera* has been beaten and dragged through my city like an animal. I want to roar to the heavens and burn the men where they stand careless with their hands on her.

"My prince," a man says from just in front of Nera. "I have brought this Fae thief here to be tried by you." He stands tall and proud, and I recognize the sharp lines of his aged face. He is the panther shifter that owns the manor where I left Nera all those years ago. He is her host. "This girl has been working in my home since she was a child, and she has been stealing food from my family and escaping into the forbidden Night Woods. The punishment for this is death."

Fury ripples through my body as I take a step toward the man. I could kill him right here and now. "Standing for my father, I believe it is me who decides what her punishment shall be, is it not?" It's a struggle not to shout the words at him.

He flinches under my gaze, and dips his head. "Yes, of course, my prince."

I look down at Nera as her head slowly rises and her eyes trail up my body until they land on my face. Recognition crosses her blue eyes, and they widen as she takes me in. A purple bruise stretches across her soft cheek, and a growl leaves my chest, just loud enough for the people closest to me to hear.

Nera's mouth drops open, but I shake my head at her. "You have proof that this girl has stolen from you, then?" I look back at the panther shifter.

He stands taller, lifting his chin in pride. "My servants have sworn to me that it is true. Just last night, the girl herself admitted to returning from the Night Woods, but she has yet to confess to her crimes of thievery."

I nod, pretending to care about a single thing this cretin has to say. "Guards," I shout, turning toward my father's men. "Take the Fae girl to the dungeons. She will spend the night there."

The men move to take Nera, and every inch of my body feels like it could burn as I watch even more hands grab onto her. Her blue eyes meet mine, and the hurt that I see in her breaks my heart just a little more.

The guards drag Nera away, and I turn my attention back to an offended-looking panther shifter. "You aren't going to kill her? She should be punished!"

I call my dragon forward and steam pours from my nose and lips. I step to the man's face and glare down at his smaller frame. "You will not question me, do you understand? Until my father returns, I am your king. Return to your home and be grateful for your life this day."

He grinds his teeth together before dipping his head once more and rushing off with his men. I left Nera with this man when she was just a child. Guilt floods me as I try to focus on the next people to approach the throne. Nera was hurt because of me. She stole food for the boy she thought I was. How can I ever forgive myself?

CHAPTER 11

NERA

This can't be real. I slump against the dungeon wall beneath the castle, my body cold and shaking. It's dark down here, the smell of rust and mold permeates the air.

I feel like I'm trapped in a never ending nightmare. This dream started out with a kiss that ended in heartbreak, and now everything I thought I've known for seven years is a lie.

I close my eyes and remember the night the golden dragon saved me from freezing to death. It was almost a year before I saw that same dragon flying above the city while I was out with Teyla at the market. I was in awe of his golden scales and large wings.

I asked Teyla who the dragon was, and she told me only one person in the entire city had golden scales. The eldest dragon prince, son of King Iredras. I never knew his name, but I knew without a doubt that he was the one who took me from the Night Woods.

But could my dragon savior be the same boy that I meet each month in those very woods? I shake my head, gripping my hair and feeling like I've lost my mind. It can't be true.

"Girl," a deep male voice speaks from the dark dungeon outside my cell door. "Rise for Prince Reinor Iredras."

Reinor's name rings through my head. He gave me his true name, but that's the only truth I ever got from him.

I stand, shaking in my nightgown that has been ripped from being dragged from my bed this morning. I cross my arms over my chest, forcing the shivers back so I don't look weak, even though it's much too late for that.

The guard outside my cell steps to the side, allowing Reinor to move into the dim light. His face is so familiar to me. I know his golden-brown eyes like I know my own reflection. The soft stubble of his face is as dark as his brown hair that hangs in its usual way over thick eyebrows. His lips are pressed into a thin line as he studies me, where a warm smile usually rests.

"Your highness," I rasp out, my throat too tight to speak. I bow slightly to the prince of the City of Shifters, and he growls low at my gesture.

Reinor turns to his guard, resting a gloved hand on his shoulder. "Please leave us. I wish to talk to the prisoner alone."

The guard hesitates before walking away. "She could possess the magic of the Fae, my prince. Maybe I should—"

Reinor blows out dark smoke from his mouth, his dragon fire threatening to be released as he spins on his guard. "She is *not* dangerous! Go!" The guard dips his head before running from the dungeon without another word.

I take a step toward the bars, holding my head high. "I could be dangerous. Isn't that why I'm here in *your* dungeon?"

Reinor steps to the cell door and quickly unlocks it before ripping it open. His gaze threatens to melt me as he enters my cell. "I know you, Nera. You don't belong here."

I scoff, anger overcoming me. "You know me?" I look him up and down, the boy I thought I knew dressed in an expensive tunic, a heavy cloak, and embroidered pants. "Well, I don't know you at all, do I?"

He raises his hands, reaching for me, but I step back against the stone wall. "Nera, please try to understand. Let me get you out of this cell." His jaw ticks with frustration. "You *do* know me, I promise."

I shake my head, wrapping my arms around myself to stop my shivering. "You don't know what a promise is, *dragon* prince." I spit the words at him, hatred replacing anything I thought I felt for this man just a day ago. "You told me you were human. I worried for you being alone in those woods for years! I *stole* for you, Reinor, and I was punished for it."

He flinched, his shoulders sagging, but his own eyes show anger that matches my own. "We both lied, Nera. Do you even hear yourself?" He throws his hands in the air. "You told me you were a panther shifter, did you not?"

I can't stop my hand from shoving against his hard chest. "I lied to protect myself. My kind isn't welcome here, and you know that! But why did you lie? To continue playing whatever game you were playing with me? The spoiled prince looking for a thrill in the forbidden woods with a commoner?" I choke on my words, my throat feeling too tight from hurt.

Reinor steps closer to me, his large frame towering over my shaking body. "You don't know anything!"

"Clearly," I shout back, refusing to back down.

His jaw is tight and his eyes glow gold as they pierce me. His scent is the same one that I've grown to crave, that warm honey and bark scent that I can't wait to smell each month. How can this be *my* Reinor? No wonder he refused to run away with me. He could never love me as I love him.

"Come upstairs with me, Nera." His voice is softer as one of his hands rises to stroke my cheek. "You'll freeze down here in that gown. I'll protect you."

I try not to whimper at the delicious feeling of his warmth so close to me. I can't trust him though, even though my heart wants to give in so badly.

I shake my head and push his hand off of me. "I'll stay here where I belong." I look down at my bleeding feet against the dirty stone. "Go live your royal life, Reinor. You knew from the beginning that I didn't fit in it."

Reinor steps back as if I just slapped him. I try not to look into his eyes for fear that he'll break me down with those golden eyes.

He turns to walk away from me, pausing at the door to remove his large cloak. "Nobody can know that I let you live, Nera. Your old life is over now, so you will never return to the city." He tosses his cloak into my cell, letting it fall at my feet. "If you want to spend a night in this place, so be it. Nobody will come down here to harm you. You have my word."

I watch Reinor's feet as he stomps away from me, leaving my cell door open as he goes. Once I can't hear his footsteps any longer, I grip his cloak and throw it over my body, curling up beneath its warmth.

I let the tears fall freely, sobs wracking my body as I drown in the scent of the man I thought I loved. Seven years ago, I lost my life in the human lands, never allowed to return to my family. Now, I've lost my life amongst the shifters. I have no home, no purpose, and the only person that gave me hope in this life isn't who I thought he was. Where do I go from here?

PART 2

A FAE BORN

CHAPTER 12

NERA

Thirteen Years Old

"I cannot believe father is letting us go to the market unsupervised." Teyla's gray eyes are practically glowing, though her shifting magic is not accessible to her for at least another two years.

I don't mind that she pulls my arm to the point of pain as we run through the streets of the city. Teyla Cragore is already like a sister to me, even though her parents only allow me to live in their home as a servant. Teyla has never treated me as such, and it helps me feel at home, though my real home is a world away.

I grip my stained skirt with one hand as I attempt to keep up with Teyla. "Is the market really so exciting? In the village where I grew up, shopping wasn't all that adventurous."

Teyla smiles back at me, finally slowing her quick stride now that we are approaching the center of the City of Shifters. "It's not the place that's exciting, Nera. It is the fact that we are not stuck at home. Being here, away from my parents, we can almost feel a sense of freedom." She spins in her brand new dress, the smooth fabric shining under the summer sun.

I can't stop my own grin as I watch her so carefree. "You're right. I guess I just worry that the other shifters will see me as I truly am."

I make sure to fix my dark hair so it hides my pointed Fae ears from the shifters. My kind are not welcome in this city. Sometimes I feel like I am not welcome anywhere.

"You are a beautiful young woman, Nera. That is all they will see." She loops her arm with mine as we approach the bustling market at the center of town.

My eyes widen as I take in the sight of the incredible market. Shops of all kinds form a wide circle around an imposing statue at the center of everything. The statue depicts a mighty dragon with his mouth opened wide as he breathes fire toward the sky. Surrounding the dragon is a cobbled stone street with people moving in all directions, coming and going as they spend the day shopping or browsing the market.

Nobody looks twice at me or Teyla, and the pressure in my chest eases. I look off to the right of the city where the street curves up toward the mighty castle that watches over the shifters. I've heard that the royal family of dragon shifters lives in the castle, and they will occasionally come down to visit the people on days like today, when the sun is shining and the city is busy.

"Do you think we'll get to see the dragons?" I ask, leaning close to Teyla.

She shrugs and tugs me toward a shop with sparkling jewels hanging in the windows. "I've never seen the royal family up close, but sometimes they fly over the city in their dragon form."

"Why don't they fly toward the woods, over your home? I'd love to see a real dragon." I have never told Teyla of the dragon that rescued me from the Night Woods a year ago. I'm still unsure if the whole thing was a dream.

Teyla pauses to give me a stern look. "*Our* home, Nera. You are family." I smile, though I know it's not true. "But, the dragons avoid the forbidden woods. I hate living so far out of the city. Nobody wants to come over there."

The Cragore's manor is a beautiful home that rests on land that my parents would have loved owning, but it does border the Night Woods, which are strictly forbidden to enter. Many of the shifters avoid even getting close to the area which gives the Cragores ultimate privacy, but also makes Teyla feel like an outcast. I don't mind so much.

Teyla pulls me with her into a jewelry shop that makes my mouth fall open. The whole store sparkles with the many different stones and jewels lining the walls.

I tug on my friend's arm. "We cannot buy anything in here, Teyla. These are much too expensive."

Teyla grins evilly at me. "Father doesn't know that I have been saving my allowance. I was meant to buy school books with the money, but the librarian gave me the books I needed for free." She grabs both of my hands in hers. "I want to buy you something."

I stare in awe at her. "Oh, no. You can't do that. Buy yourself something, Tey."

Teyla shakes her head, her pink cheeks rising with her kind smile. "I have always wanted a sister, Nera. When you came into my life, I could not have been happier." Her smile falls slightly. "My parents treat you as a slave, and you are given almost nothing. You deserve happiness, okay?"

I blink back the tears in my eyes as I nod. "Thank you for making me feel like I still have a family, Teyla."

She pulls me into a tight embrace before spinning me around so I'm forced to look at a wall of necklaces. "Now, these are not normal jewels. They are enchanted by the sorcerers in the cities beside Elf Mountain. Their magic is capable of healing wounds, concealing one's appearance, or giving the ability of interacting in one's dreams. I've heard that some of the gems will call out to the person that is meant to own it." She waves a hand at the wall. "Do any of these stand out to you?"

I scan the many jewels, gems, and stones. Each is unique, and they all rest at the end of a chain, meant to be worn as a necklace. Could I even get away with wearing one of these without Mr. or Mrs. Cragore knowing? It will need to be small.

My eyes stop on a specific necklace, and I cannot take my gaze away from it. I reach out and touch the shining gold gem that is smaller than my pinky nail and resting in the eye of a bronze dragon pendant. The entire thing captivates me, and I can't explain why.

"This one," I whisper, feeling a connection to the piece.

"Great choice," a female voice speaks from across the small shop. An older woman with silver hair and a dress made of more patterns than my mind can comprehend approaches us. "This is one of the very few Fae pieces that I sell in my store."

Teyla gasps. "You mean, this is not elven?"

The woman shakes her head. "Before the fall of the Faerie kingdom, I would often trade with their jewelers. It has been many years since our kind have had contact with the Fae, but I still have some of their enchanted necklaces." She grabs the dragon necklace and hands it to me. "This is one of them."

I gaze down at the golden dragon eye. "What is the enchantment on this necklace?"

The jeweler woman touches my arm gently. "This dragon is a sign of destiny. As long as you wear this necklace close to your skin, you will always be led to your true destiny. It is a comfort to know that everything happens for a reason and you are on the right path. If you ever feel like you aren't heading to your happy ending, touch this dragon and know that you will get there."

"We're getting it," Teyla says beside me. She hands the woman a small purse full of coins, but the woman refuses the payment.

"I can't take your money for this piece. I have never seen a person so perfectly chosen by a pendant as you have been." She stares deep into my eyes. "It was made for you, dear. Cherish it."

I nod, in awe of the woman's kindness. "Thank you so much. I will never forget this."

Teyla and I make our way outside the shop, and Teyla hurries to hook the dragon pendant around my neck. "It really was made for you, Nera."

I open my mouth to speak, but the sound of a loud roar fills the sky above us. I jerk my head back in time to see a gorgeous golden dragon fly over us, its shining scales flashing the sun into my eyes. My heart races and my mind returns to that night in the woods a year ago.

It has to be the same dragon that saved me from near death and brought me to Teyla's doorstep. "Who is that?" I ask, completely in awe.

Teyla watches the dragon with me. "That is the dragon prince. I've heard that he is the only dragon with his coloring in centuries. He is still young, but he is heir to the throne."

I swallow hard and my heart sinks. He can't be the dragon that saved me, unless the dragon prince was somehow out in the forbidden woods on his own. It's not likely, though. Still, I clutch the dragon around my neck and feel a sense of peace as I watch the prince fly back to his castle.

"So, I still have my allowance to spend." Teyla nudges my arm, bringing my attention back to her. "Shall we go spend it on truffles and pastries and make ourselves sick?"

I laugh along with her and loop my arm through hers. "Yes, please."

CHAPTER 13

NERA
Now

I shiver violently against the cold stone floor, pulling Reinor's cloak tighter around my quaking body. I hate it down here in this disgusting dungeon, but it was my own choice to stay instead of going with the man who betrayed me.

I groan and stuff my face in the delicious scent of the cloak, willing my stomach not to growl in the empty room. *Warm honey and tree bark.*

"Ugh, I'm such an idiot," I whisper to myself, wishing I could just go back to yesterday morning when Reinor asked me to stay upstairs in the castle.

I know why I chose to stay behind, though. How can I go up there and live with people who wish me dead? I can't even trust the one person that I have relied on for the past seven years. Every part of my soul feels broken, beaten, and altogether shattered.

I curl up on my side and reach to my upper arm that is covered by the thin fabric of my nightgown. The delicate chain that holds my dragon pendant is tied securely around me, hidden from sight as always. If my host family had ever found out about the jewelry, they would have taken it from me instantly.

I undo the clasp and hang the chain around my neck, letting the golden dragon rest against the skin of my chest. I'm instantly filled with a new sense of comfort and hope as I gaze down at my dragon.

"How is this a part of my destiny, huh?" I ask the golden eye of the creature. "Where do I go from here?"

No answer comes from the jewel, as it never has, but footsteps alert me to another person in the dungeon, and I sit upright, ready to defend against whatever is here for me. An older woman, not elderly, with tall pointed ears longer than my Fae ones, steps into the dim light coming through the sliver of window above me.

She smiles down at me through hanging curls of hair that fall from a loose red bun on her head. Her eyes are a bright green, unnaturally so. My eyes immediately widen at the sight of two sharp fangs in her mouth, and my whole body goes on alert.

"Do not be frightened by my fangs, dear girl. All elves have the same teeth as myself. It is simply a defense mechanism." She kneels before me just inside my cell, likely dirtying her nice dress skirts. "I will not harm you, Nera."

An elf? I didn't know elves were welcome in the City of Shifters.

I sit with my shoulders back and my chin held high. I can't show weakness, even if this woman is being kind. "Why are you here?" I can only assume Reinor gave her my name and sent her down here.

She smiles again, and I try not to balk at how sweet and equally terrifying the look is. "My name is Lanya. I am normally a cleaning maid in this castle, but I got a raise today. Prince Reinor has named me your personal lady's maid and sent me here to bring you to your room."

I shake my head. "I am not a lady, ma'am. I am a servant, and I am fine to stay right where I'm at." Even as I say the words, I ache to go with Lanya to a comfortable bedroom, preferably after a long bath and a meal.

Lanya raises an eyebrow at me, her soft skin and high cheekbones giving her an otherworldly kind of beauty that I assume comes from being an elf. "My prince has informed me that you are in fact a lady and must receive the highest quality of care. He also mentioned that my lady would be stubborn and insolent." She holds up her hands. "His words, not mine. Though, I can see that he may be correct."

My jaw drops. "I am not insolent, nor am I stubborn!" *Well, not always.* "Maybe *your* prince is merely an ass!"

I cover my mouth in shock as Lanya's shining eyes widen. I probably shouldn't have said that about the heir to the shifter throne, and the realization hits me that I could be executed for such a thing.

Even more surprise floods me as Lanya releases a soft laugh that wrinkles her eyes at the edges. "It seems you know Reinor quite well. I suspected as much, though he gave me very little information about your... relationship."

I scoff. "There is no relationship. He is a liar who stuck me down here to rot." Hurt pierces my heart all over again.

Lanya reaches a hand out and lays her palm against my knee. Her nails are like claws, but I'm not afraid or worried that they'll pierce me. "Come with me, Nera. No matter how you feel about the prince, let me take care of you. You are hungry, and you have been hurt in more ways than one. Rotting and freezing to death in a dungeon cell will do you no good."

The cold beneath me seems to just seep farther into my bones, making the final decision for me. I nod and stand, letting Lanya take my hand in hers. "I will go with you, but I refuse to speak with Reinor."

She tugs me through the dungeon and up a skinny flight of stone stairs. "No problem. I will tell him that you request some space."

"Can you tell him that I request to never see or speak to him again?"

Lanya chuckles warmly, opening a heavy wooden door into an ornate hallway. "Oh, dear. I don't believe he would appreciate that so much, but I will try to give him the hint without hurting his pride too badly."

I pull Reinor's long cloak tighter around my body as we exit the hallway into what looks to be a main sitting room of the castle. Anyone could see me in this room, and I don't wish to show the world my thin nightgown. *Well, not again at least.*

Lanya takes me up two flights of stairs and through so many hallways and doorways that I get easily turned around. Thankfully, we reach the bedroom chosen for me before I have to run into any other being. Particularly one dragon prince.

"Here we are, my lady."

I step into the open bedroom and my jaw drops. This is no ordinary guest bedroom. The large canopy-covered bed against the far wall is covered in plush bedding and at least six fluffy pillows. A large rug with gold and pink accents takes up the majority of the wooden floor, and the natural light pouring in through a floor-to-ceiling window gives me an incredible view of the mountain canyon behind the castle.

Various paintings and expensive furniture decorate the walls, giving the entire space a cozy feel. Lanya steps through a door that blends with the wall off to my right. I follow her into a beautiful washroom with wide counters and a massive porcelain tub that is filled to the brim with steaming water. A clean towel and a change of clothes sits beside the tub waiting for me.

"Did you prepare this before coming to get me?" I ask Lanya, glancing her way. She nods. "You were so sure I'd agree to come up here that you spent the time heating and filling the bath?"

Lanya smiles and waves her long fingers in my direction. Soft light drifts from her fingertips as she drops her hand into the water and the surface begins boiling and then settling to a warm steam once again.

"I am an elf, Nera. I possess magic that the shifters you know are not capable of. Why do you think the shifter king keeps me around?"

I shake my head in awe. "I wish I understood magic better. It's incredible."

She takes my hand in hers. "You are Fae, which means you have magic of your own. The Fae are capable of incredible enchantments, very different from the elves' elemental magic." She tilts her head at me. "Did your family not teach you of your gifts?"

I drop my gaze to the floor. "I have no family."

Lanya is silent for a long moment before she clears her throat and steps back toward the bedroom. "Please, clean yourself up and get some rest, my lady. I will return in an hour with dinner."

I smile back at her with a dip of my head. "Thank you, Lanya."

CHAPTER 14

REINOR

I can't keep pacing like this. I need to swallow my pride and go in there to talk to her. I pause my back-and-forth stomping to look back at the door that takes me from my bedroom and into the hallway outside of Nera's new room.

Yes, I chose to place her just across the hall from me for many reasons. My rooms are at the opposite end of the castle from my father's and my brother's. I can keep a better eye on her this way. And, maybe I'm hoping that I can run into her more often if she's so close to me. Not to mention that I can hear her movements if I listen really close.

"Oh gods, help me," I mutter. I grip my head and try to force myself to stay put. "She doesn't want to see you, Reinor. She asked to be left alone."

I scoff and throw my hands on my hips. "She also chose to spend the damn night in a cell rather than be anywhere near me. She's clearly lost her mind."

I growl before pushing through my bedroom door and stopping just outside Nera's door. I take a steadying breath as I knock on the wood and wait for her to answer. The door pulls open just a crack and familiar blue eyes peer through at me. I can hear her low groan of disappointment before she tugs the door all the way open and her blue eyes change to a bright shade of gray.

What does gray mean?

"What do you want, Reinor?" She holds the steady gray gaze at me.

I straighten my shoulders, trying to ignore the damp waves of black hair that fall over her narrow shoulders and the way that new gown hugs every one of her curves. She looks...well. *Tell her she looks beautiful. Tell her you're glad she came upstairs.*

"Is that any way to greet your prince and current acting king?" *Or that.* I let the words fall out with a pompousness I was unaware that I possessed.

Nera's eyebrows raise high as she purses her pink lips. "Oh, I am so sorry, your highness. I never meant any offense." She curtsies sweetly, but her eyes threaten certain death.

I sigh and roll my eyes. "You don't have to call me that, Nera. I didn't mean–"

She holds a hand up to stop me. "Are you not Prince Reinor Iredras, heir to the king of shifter-kind? Apparently acting-king for some reason?"

I bite the inside of my lip. "Yes, I am. But–"

She cuts me off again, and angry heat fills my chest. "Then, I have no right to call you anything that any other prisoner cannot. I am your prisoner, right?"

I step closer to her, letting that tantalizingly familiar scent flood me. "No, you are *not* my prisoner. You are my guest."

Nera's gray eyes return to their light blue as she looks up at me. For a moment, I see the girl in the woods that I have known for many years. "If I am your guest, I can leave whenever I wish?"

I ache to touch her, but I keep my hands to myself. "I can't let you go into the city. It's too dangerous." She doesn't understand what could happen to both of us if the shifters found out I had a faerie in my home, or that I spared her after she chose to steal and lie.

"I've heard of your father's temper, and his dislike for the other kingdoms. I'm in as much danger here as I am out there." She crosses her arms over her chest, and my eyes fall to the golden dragon pendant that rests between her breasts.

"Why do you wear that?" I ask, curiosity distracting me. I've never seen this on her before.

Nera pulls her dress higher in the front, shielding the jewel. "It was a gift, and none of your business."

"It's a golden dragon…like me." Does she know I'm the only one like myself?

I meet her gaze, but she keeps her face hard and unfeeling. "I was rescued from certain death by a golden dragon once." She pauses just before looking away from me. "That was a different lifetime though."

"I should have told you then who I was, Nera." I reach out to touch her cheek, but she steps away.

Her hand moves to the door. "Yes, you should have," she says softly before shutting the door in my face.

I catch the wood before it can click shut. "My father will not welcome you here, and the city will wish to see you executed. Stay in this wing of the castle and do not speak to anyone other than me and Lanya. You're stuck with me until I can find another way to protect you. Give me a week."

"So, a prisoner," she mutters softly. Nera looks through the crack of the door and nods once. "Fine, but leave me alone until then."

With that, the door clicks shut and I am left staring at the piece of wood, my heart feeling lost. Nera may never look at me the way she did the moment she kissed me in the Night Woods, but I won't give up on giving her the future she deserves. I will make sure she finds her freedom one way or another.

CHAPTER 15

REINOR

I shuffle down the velvet-covered stairs toward the den. My father's right-hand, Thomin, is sitting on a plush chair awaiting my arrival.

"I am glad you decided to wake up this morning, my prince." His tone hints at his teasing nature.

Thomin has been working for my father since before I was born. He is like a parent to me and Calder, always keeping us in line. Unlike our father, though, Thomin is kind to us. Owl shifters like him are incredibly loyal and kind-hearted. While Dad was always grumbling and growling, Thomin was there with a smile and sage advice.

"I'm sorry, Thomin. I've been unable to sleep well the past few nights." I run my hand down my face, not caring to hide the exhaustion in my face.

He raises a thick gray eyebrow at me, highlighting his old age. "Could it be the fae girl that is keeping you up all hours of the night? You know, a king needs his rest."

I scoff. "I'm no king, Thomin. I'm just a fill-in." I skip over his comment about Nera. He wouldn't understand the relationship I have with her.

Thomin rises from his seat with grace, and not even a hint of a wobble even though he could be my great grandfather. "You're not a king today, but you will be in the future. No time like the present to act the part, eh?"

The urge to roll my eyes is strong, but I hold back. I move to sit on the couch and settle in for a morning of Thomin's debriefing when the den door swings open and slams against the wall beside it.

My best friend, Elex, steps into the room with my brother thrown over his wide shoulder. He lays Calder on the empty sofa, and I rush to my brother's side. "What the hell is going on, Elex?"

Elex brushes off his dirty tunic and wipes a bead of sweat from his dark brow. "One of the gate guards found Calder passed out in the garden half an hour ago. I was coming in to see you when I spotted the fox shifter guard dragging Calder's heavy ass across the yard. The poor guy was nearly buckling over from the weight of a dragon on his back."

I swipe the hair away from Calder's closed eyes and check his pulse. "His heart is barely beating." I stand and turn to Elex. "Go get Lanya as fast as you can."

My friend nods without any argument and runs with wolf speed out of the den. I spin back to Thomin. "Can you do anything for him? What do you think happened?"

Thomin leans over Calder's still body and he touches his burning hot forehead. He sniffs the air around my brother, and the skin around his nose scrunches up in disgust. "He reeks of alcohol. He must have drank more than he could handle."

"That's it? Too much drink? He looks halfway in the grave!" I yell, unable to control the overwhelming fear I have for my little brother.

Calder may be every bit as evil-hearted as our father, but he's still my family. I would still do just about anything to protect him. *Stupid me.*

Thomin unbuttons Calder's sweat-stained shirt, letting the cool air of the room calm his hot skin. "Alcohol poisoning can be deadly, Reinor. This is very serious."

"He's right," Lanya's voice drifts into the room like a soft melody.

For a woman with dagger-sharp teeth and claws that can slice you open, she brings peace with her wherever she goes. Lanya drops to her knees beside me, letting her palms explore my brother. She closes her bright green eyes and focuses silently as her hands rove Calder from his head to his belly. I remain quiet so I don't disturb her magic.

"He drank way more than his body is meant to handle, even for a dragon shifter. I'm surprised he's still breathing." Lanya looks at me with sadness on her face. "I can't stop the poisoning on his brain, but I can lessen his fever and draw the poison from within him out through his skin."

I shake my head. "But, what will happen to his brain if you can't stop the damage of the alcohol?"

Lanya bites on the inside of her cheek and lowers her gaze to Calder. "He will become brain-dead, and never wake up again."

NERA

If I sit in that room for even one more minute, I'll lose my mind. I need to move, to run. Anything to stop feeling so trapped. For an elaborately built and expensive building, this castle can feel so much like a prison.

I know nothing of where each of these hallways lead. Reinor demanded that I remain in the west wing, but he didn't so much as give me a tour or even quick directions. I have no idea where one wing ends and another begins.

The halls are dark, especially for the morning hours. My slippered feet make almost no sound as I tip-toe past a wall of framed images. Landscapes surrounding the City of Shifters that I recognize, and many that I don't, are painted on the canvases. The images are expertly done, and I want to stop to appreciate them, until voices filter toward me.

My pointed ears perk up, and I make my way down the hall to stop just outside a large door. I know I shouldn't be eavesdropping, but I know nothing of Reinor or his royal family, and I am not about to ask him anything. I can't even look at the man without my blood boiling in anger.

I press my ear to the wood, instantly recognizing Lanya's panicked voice. "He drank way more than his body is meant to handle, even for a dragon shifter. I'm surprised he's still breathing. I can't stop the poisoning on his brain, but I can lessen his fever and draw the poison from within him out through his skin."

My heart sinks and a lump clogs my throat as I imagine Reinor lying there sick and dying. Darkness clouds my vision and I sink to the floor, a throbbing ache growing behind my eyes. Then, just as quickly as the emotions overcame me, they wash away as I hear Reinor's voice follow Lanya's.

"But, what will happen to his brain if you can't stop the damage of the alcohol?"

He's okay. It's not him. Why do I even care?

Lanya speaks again. "He will become brain-dead, and never wake up again."

Something thuds against a hard surface and Reinor's roar of anger vibrates through the air. "Dammit, Calder!" He shouts and I can hear his stomping footsteps on the ground. His voice comes again, softer than before. "Do what you can for him, Lanya."

"Yes, my prince." Lanya goes quiet, and a new energy fills the air. I know it must be coming from whatever Lanya is doing to the injured person, but I can feel it like thick smoke as it floats through the heavy door.

I wait in silence for someone to say something, and a new voice finally startles me. It's a man, possibly elderly with the rasp of age that fills the tone. "What can we do for the prince if you cannot stop the damage to his brain? We cannot let him die."

The prince? Reinor's brother then.

"I know of only one other possibility, but it's a long shot," Lanya says quietly.

Reinor's voice rises again. "Tell us. I'll try anything." His voice is full of an ache I've never heard from him before. Of course, how much have I really, truly seen of him?

I want to curl up in my own self-pity again, until Lanya says my name. "Nera may be able to help him."

"What? How?" Reinor asks.

"Elf magic is powerful, and I can heal many injuries, but the Fae are on another level when it comes to healing magicks."

"Nera was not raised with a Fae family. She may not have any magic at all." Reinor knows me better than I know him.

A feminine sigh fills the air from Lanya. "All Elves, and all Fae have magic inside of them. They just need to learn how to use it. I can try and guide her." The room is silent for a long moment before Lanya speaks again. "There is no other way to save the prince. He will never wake again if Nera cannot heal him."

Reinor clears his throat. "I won't ask her, Lanya. Besides, she would never do this for my family. She hates me."

A small twinge sparks in my heart at the sadness filling Reinor's voice. He believes that I hate him enough to let his brother die…and maybe I do hate Reinor, but I'm not a monster.

I square my shoulders and twist the door handle before pushing my way into the large den. My eyes take in the two strangers standing behind a sofa where Reinor and Lanya

91

kneel beside the body of an unconscious man about my age.

All eyes turn to me as I try to present myself as confident and unworried. "I will do what I can to help the prince," I announce, not looking at anyone but Lanya. "Tell me what I must do."

CHAPTER 16

NERA

Lanya's bright green eyes look toward me with something akin to pride. She stands from beside the sick man and she takes my hands gently in hers, quickly retracting her long claws before doing so.

I gasp. "I didn't know you could retract your claws."

"We can't just go around accidentally cutting into everything we touch now, can we?" Her smiling lips drop as her gaze locks with mine. "Have you ever used magic before, my lady?"

I push past the formal name as I shake my head. "No, I didn't even know my kind had magic. I was raised by humans."

Movement makes me look up at Reinor where he watches me with surprise on his handsome face. "You were raised in the Mortal Lands?"

"Now isn't the time, your highness." I don't wait to catch his reaction to my bitter tone as I look back at Lanya. "How do I use this Fae magic? To be honest, I may not have any at all."

Lanya shakes her head. "I can feel it in you, my dear. You have a great deal of power deep inside of you. A magic that you have been unknowingly protecting from prying eyes."

My mind flashes back to a memory from many years ago. The fortune teller woman that I saw at the fair said something similar to me. *"Protect your magic, and your heart, but also know that your heart will not be solely yours forever. There are so many trials ahead of you, but you were born to survive, and you are more than what eyes are able to see."*

I'm more than what eyes can see, and I *do* have Fae magic. I nod to Lanya. "Okay, I'm ready." I follow her as she again kneels beside the man. "Who is he?" I ask, studying his face.

His dark brown hair is shaggy and damp, pushed to the side by soothing hands. He has a strong jaw that's cleanly shaven, but his eyes are surrounded by sunken-in circles. If I hadn't heard them call him a prince, I would have still known this was Reinor's brother, just from the resemblance alone.

"My younger brother," Reinor says, drawing my attention to him as he sits on the floor beside me. "His name is Calder, and he must have been out all night drinking with his friends. He has alcohol poisoning."

"He was passed out in the gardens outside," another man says. He stands behind the couch, his hands behind his back as he stands like a soldier. This man is tall like Reinor, and similar in age, but lighter in coloring and with dark blue eyes.

"I am Nera," I say, stretching my hand out in greeting to the man. "And you are?"

He dips his head to me and takes my hand into his warm one. "Elex Minara, Sword Master to the king and friend of the family."

The older man beside him takes my hand next. His touch is soft and gentle. "And my name is Thomin, right hand to the king. Please do what you can to help our youngest prince."

"I will," I say. I lay a hand on Calder's chest and turn toward Lanya again.

"Okay, Nera. What I need you to do first is close your eyes and place both of your hands on each side of Calder's head." I do as she says. "Now, focus on him, and nothing else. Clear your mind of all distractions. Can you feel Calder's living spirit?"

I try to focus on where my skin touches Calder's. I feel warmth, moisture from his sweat, and if I try to feel deeper, I can almost feel a pulsing sort of energy separate from the physical.

I nod. "I can't say for sure, but I think I feel it."

"Good," Lanya says softly. "Now, focus on the same type of energy inside of yourself. Once you find it, you can classify it as your own spirit, your Fae spirit."

I find what she says, and my body suddenly feels open and exposed. "I don't like the way that feels," I say, keeping my eyes closed and my hands on Calder's head.

I can feel a warm hand rest against my lower back, and by the weight and size of it, it has to be Reinor. I choose to not push him away, and accept his comfort instead. I may need it.

Lanya shifts beside me, and I can feel her closer. "Your magic is contained within your spirit, Nera. You have been hiding it for years, so exposing it like this will feel wrong and maybe even slightly painful, but you must do it."

I nod. "I'm okay, just tell me how to wield it."

"Now that you've located your own spirit, try to open it up. You do this in your own way, whatever feels right. Get inside that ball of energy and you will know when you find the magic. It will reach out to you once it's no longer trapped, and it will overwhelm you for a moment."

I don't really understand what she means, but I follow her instructions anyway. In my mind, I reach out to my spirit, and I grasp it on both sides with imaginary hands. I break the ball open easily and my whole world instantly glows so bright that I am momentarily blinded, even in my mind.

I gasp and fall backwards, away from Calder. I don't hit the ground as something envelopes me in warmth, cradling my shaking body. Someone calls out my name, but it's a distant sound floating on the wind.

In an instant, my eyes fly open and I'm staring up into shining golden eyes. The shaking in my limbs fades, and my heartbeat settles back into a normal rhythm.

"Nera," Reinor says gently. His eyes are shining gold like his dragon's, but as I stare into them, dazed and confused, they begin to fade to their normal golden-brown. "Can you hear me? Are you hurt?"

I shake my head and look down at where Reinor is holding me close to his chest and stroking his long fingers against my arm. I quickly push myself out of his grasp.

"What are you doing?" I ask him, accusation in my voice. I shouldn't be upset with him right now, but some part of me can't let it go.

Reinor sits back, eyebrows raised, and his brown eyes scan my face before he shakes his head. "Nothing. You just started to glow and then you fell over. I—I'm sorry." His eyes fall from me, but not before I catch the hurt in them.

I look down at my hands and my eyes open wide. I really am glowing. "This is my magic?" I turn toward Lanya and she nods to me. "How do I use it to heal Calder?"

Lanya takes my hands again and places them back on Calder's head. "Close your eyes once more and find that spirit inside of Calder. It should be able to show you where he has been injured. Push your light into that spot of him, and if you feel the need to take from it, do so. Let your gut guide you."

I close my eyes and begin to search once more for Calder's spirit. The orb is bright, glowing like my magic.

One spot, though, has gone dark. It looks void of life and light. It has to be the spot that's injured.

I mentally push my magic into the dark part of the orb, and the spot begins to glow again. Something thick and black coats the orb where my magic can't reach. I trust in my gut and the urge I have to drag that inky spot away from him like slurping it through a straw until every last bit is gone and only light remains.

"Nera, that's enough. You must stop."

I open my eyes and the den spins around me as I wobble into Lanya's side. She grabs onto me and hoists me to my feet.

"You did well, Nera. I believe you healed his brain completely."

I try to focus my gaze on Lanya, but spots cloud my vision. "I don't feel well."

Lanya's cold hands stroke my cheek. "You have never used magic before. It will take time to learn to not drain yourself so fast. Rest now, my dear."

My eyes close as I sink into Lanya's arms, but I can still hear Reinor's voice. "Let me take her to her room." Warm hands rest on my shoulders, but they're quickly removed.

Lanya speaks again. "It'll be best if I take her, my prince." She lifts me into her small but strong arms. "Look after your brother."

CHAPTER 17

REINOR

I stand at Nera's bedroom door, my hands feeling raw from how many times I've rubbed them together out of worry this past day.

After Nera healed Calder yesterday morning, he improved rapidly. He awoke with fresh eyes just an hour later, asking what happened and ready to take on the world. I not-so-kindly told him that he was being an idiot and nearly drank himself to death.

Calder didn't take the news well, storming off and ignoring me for the rest of the day. Thanks to Elex keeping a close eye on him, I know that he has stayed home and safe since the incident. Small miracles I suppose.

As for Nera, I have no idea how she is doing since using her power for the first time. She looked so tired and spent after healing my no-good brother that I regretted letting her do it, and my disdain for Calder grew just a little more for it. Now, I'm so tired of sitting back and waiting for Lanya's sparse news on how Nera is doing.

I knock on the wood and wait for a long minute, listening to the sound of water sloshing and bare footsteps slapping against the polished flooring before Nera swings the door open and greets me with wet hair and a damp nightgown that does little to hide her curvy frame.

Gods help me.

Nera huffs and turns to lift a towel from her bed. She flips her hair upside down and begins drying the dark strands, not caring even slightly that I'm watching the whole display. "What are you doing here, Reinor?" She flips her head back and her blue eyes pierce me.

I look her up and down, unable to stop myself. "Were you having a bath?"

Nera gestures to her wet hair and clingy nightgown. "Isn't it obvious?" *Damn that attitude.* "Hot baths are a luxury that I was never given at the Cragore's house. I have been enjoying them."

The Cragore's I now realize are not the sweet, loving panther shifters that I thought they were for many years. Watching Mr. Cragore try to convince me to execute Nera was enough to give me that glimpse that Nera always hid, and enough to spark a new level of hatred for the panthers.

I step into her bedroom and ignore the angry glare that she throws my way. "I wanted to check in on you. To see if you're better after yesterday."

Nera's eyes soften as she nods. "Yes, I rested and now I'm back to normal. I wasn't expecting the magic to knock me down like that."

"Me neither. You gave me a scare." I try to smile down at Nera, but her eyes quickly shift away.

She turns away from me, and I want nothing more than to reach out and pull her close, to make her see me. For years in those woods it was just Nera and Reinor. We had no family, no social rank, and no worries. We only had each other's company. I've heard Nera laugh more times than I can count, and smelled her sweet scent on the breeze, floating toward me as if it were meant for only me to breathe in.

And now we are strangers.

I take another step toward her, unable to stop my own feet. "Nera, will you talk to me? Can we—"

She whirls around, her blazing eyes now flickering from gray, to black, to green. "I can't, Reinor. I don't know you anymore, and I don't think I can ever trust you again." Her words spill out in a rush, and each one hits me like a stone thrown at my chest.

"We both lied, Nera. We both needed that escape with one another each month. We *can* move past it!" I don't mean to yell, but my voice rises with each sentence.

Nera steps toward me until her scent slams against my body and wraps itself around me. So close that I can see the soft freckles on her cheeks. "Yes, I lied to you. Do you even want to know the truth, Reinor? To truly know who I am?"

I nod, my fists clenching in frustration. "Yes, of course I do! That is all I want."

Her eyes flash an ominous black at me as she starts to flood me with information. "I was abandoned in the Night Woods when I was born. I was found by the best, most caring human family in the world. I was theirs, and they were my everything." Her voice cracks. "They raised me with their son, and he was my brother in every way that mattered. I loved him. I hid my ears and kept my eyes from changing in public, all so the humans wouldn't know I was Fae. But they found out, and they tried to kill me."

My heart stutters for her as she continues in a rush. "I was forced to run from my home and back into those damned woods! I ran and ran for days until I was starving and freezing, ready to die there in the dark, alone."

The memory of that day when I flew into the woods and found Nera flash through my mind. She was so small and weak. Her fingers and toes were almost frost bitten, and she couldn't stay awake long enough to even raise her head. I warmed her by a fire and held her until her body stopped shaking. This lost girl that I didn't know.

Nera pokes me in the chest. "You came to me then. This huge, magnificent dragon. Until that day, magic and shifters were all just tales. I was half-dead but I was also in awe." Her eyes sparkle green at me and I want to stare into them for hours. They change to gray too fast. "You might have thought you were saving me when you dropped me at the Cragores' doorstep, but it was just a new kind of hell."

I swallow hard, wanting to beg Nera not to continue. I don't want to know what those people did to her, but I *need* to. "They hated me for being a faerie. They called me "thing" and "creature". They made me their servant, and anytime I messed something up, I was beaten." I growl low at her words, wishing I could go back to the other day and tear that man's hands off for ever laying them on Nera. "I had only two good things in my life. One was their daughter, Teyla. She was a true sister to me these past years, and I will always love her." She blinks back tears as she avoids my eyes once more.

I reach out to touch Nera's cheek, but she steps out of my reach. She wipes at her eyes, clearing the wetness. "And the other thing was you." She stares deep into my eyes, stopping my breath completely. "You were my solace, that something that I looked forward to each month. Running into those woods and seeing you there was *everything* to me…"

I step forward again, blocking her between me and her bed. "That's how I felt too, Nera. All I wanted was to get to you, I counted down the days each month."

She shakes her head. "You were running from a castle, from a life of privilege. I was running from lashes against my back and screams at me that I'm not good enough."

Her words slice through my chest like knives. "I never knew they were treating you that way, I swear! I wish you would've told me. Things could have been different."

Nera's hands land on my chest and my heart rate quickens. "What would you have done, Reinor? You were running from your own life, playing pretend with the Fae girl. I *stole* food for you, thinking you needed it. You lied so that you could keep your little slice of freedom."

"That's not—" I stutter, unable to explain why I lied for so long. "I may not have been physically beaten in my life, Nera, but my *privilege* is not what you believe it to be." I let my fingers touch the petal-soft skin of her cheek. "We grew to mean something to one another out there, didn't we?"

Her eyes blink up at me until the irises fade gracefully into a dark green and blue mixture. She bites on her bottom lip. "We did. The only problem, though…That man isn't who you are, Reinor Iredras. He was just a mirage."

"He is *me*, Nera." How can I get her to understand?

The air between our bodies settles, and the world goes silent. It's as if everything, down to the smallest flicker of dust, is waiting for something to happen between me and Nera. I stroke my thumb along her cheek, but all too quickly, she steps around me and walks to her bedroom door.

She places a hand on the open door. "You should go, Reinor. Your brother may need you."

"Calder is fine," I protest.

Nera waves a hand at the hall. "Please just go."

My shoulders sag, but I don't fight her on this. I walk toward the door and then out into the hall. I turn back to her one more time. "Goodnight, Nera."

She nods once and then shuts the door without a single word.

CHAPTER 18

NERA

My bare feet touch softly to the tiled kitchen floor. I only opened four wrong doors before I finally found the one I was looking for.

My stomach growls loudly in the large, dark space. "Yeah, yeah. I'm working on it," I whisper to the offended organ.

I skipped dinner tonight, my heart aching from the encounter with Reinor in my bedroom. Now, it is past midnight and my empty stomach is protesting my defiance.

Gods, having Reinor touch me the way he did, that dark longing in his golden-brown eyes. I wanted to fall into him. I wanted to give in so badly that it hurt to turn him away.

He can't feel for me the way I grew to feel for him. It's why he turned me down after our kiss in the Night Woods. He is meant to be a king, and I am meant to always be lost.

I absentmindedly touch the dragon pendant on my neck, hoping for its guidance. "Where do I go from here?" I whisper.

As usual, no answer comes to me, so I move on to the kitchen cupboards in search of something to eat. Many loaves of bread are wrapped within the cupboards, along with vegetables and bags of grain.

I tear off a chunk of bread and grab a jar of jam. It takes no time to find a knife since I know my way around a servant's kitchen better than most. I take a seat against the tall counter and spread the jam on my bread before taking the whole thing down in seconds.

Finally feeling full and settled, I turn from the kitchen and run directly into a hard chest. I Yelp and stumble backward, my eyes finding a handsome and familiar face.

"Prince Calder," I dip my head in a bow to him, hoping I'm doing it right. The dark circles are gone from around his eyes now. "You look well."

Calder eyes me curiously. "Are you that Fae girl that healed me?" His finger pokes out to touch the tip of my pointed ear. "What are you doing in my home?"

My mouth pauses half open. I don't know what to say to him. "I have, uh…been a guest in the castle this week. Did Reinor not tell you?"

His eyes open wide, but the smile that follows is so sinister that it makes my stomach turn. "No, *Reinor* didn't tell me about our…*guest*. It seems my big bro has found a dirty little secret."

I take a step back as if I've been slapped. "I don't think that's the case. It must have just slipped his mind."

"Right," Calder says, drawing out the word. He moves toward me, his broad shoulders blocking out the candle light behind him. "You don't know much about the customs in a castle, do you?"

I shake my head. "I apologize. This is new to me." I move backward again, but my back hits a stone wall. "I'll just go back to my room."

"Or you could come back to *my* room." Calder moves closer until his breath is on my face. I immediately recognize the smell of rum, and the sickness in my belly intensifies. "I like keeping secrets too, you know. Want to be one of mine?"

My jaw tightens in anger as I stare up at the inebriated man. I'm torn between cowering and attempting to run, or fighting him right here. "I'm no one's secret, sir. I'd like to go to bed now."

Calder's brown eyes darken as he reaches out and grips my arms in his strong hands. His teeth lengthen to sharp fangs, and the skin of his neck ripples with green scales quickly before they disappear once more.

"A Fae hiding within the castle walls, protected by our heir prince himself. What do you think the shifters in the city will do with news like that?" He draws in a long breath, scenting me. "I do see the appeal though."

Calder tugs me hard against his chest, knocking air out of me. I raise my knee fast, connecting with the sensitive spot between his legs. He grunts and draws back, his eyes flashing a dark green as his skin ripples with dragon scales again.

"Better creatures than you have been killed for less, faerie girl!" He raises a hand, preparing to strike me, but a roar fills the hall and something slams against Calder's side.

Calder drops to the floor with a groan. Reinor stands over his brother, his golden eyes glowing and his lip twisted into an angry snarl. "What the hell are you doing, Calder?" He shouts.

"Just playing with the castle pet, bro. Is that not why you keep her here?" Calder glares from the ground.

Reinor growls low and long, the sound of a true beast. "She is *not* yours to touch! Leave now before I end you for even *thinking* about harming my guest!"

Calder stands, puffing up his chest and looking like he may try to fight his larger brother. Smoke blows out of his nose before he flashes an angry glare my way and then stomps away from us without another word.

Reinor turns to me, his hands cupping my face in warmth. The gold in his eyes fades as he stares down at me. "Are you alright, Nera?"

I'm stunned and silent. I came looking for food and in minutes I was attacked by one prince and saved by another. What is this place?

"Nera?" Reinor asks, his voice panicked.

His eyes flick down to my mouth, and before I can protest, his lips are on mine. This kiss isn't anything like the one we shared in the Night Woods. This one is desperate and needy.

My mind registers the wildness of this moment, and I push against Reinor's chest. I move out of his grasp and I grow angry all over again.

"Is that all I am to you monsters?" I shout at Reinor, everything from the past few minutes causing me to lose my cool. "I'm a pet, something you can touch when you wish and play with it? First Calder, and now you!"

Shock and horror flashes over Reinor's handsome face. "No, Nera. That's not it at all!"

I shake my head and hold a hand up to stop him. Sure, I know Reinor isn't that person who takes advantage of people, but I don't care right now. I don't know him the way I thought I did.

"Leave me alone," I say, and I run down the hall. I know what I need. I need fresh air and starlight. I need to leave this castle.

CHAPTER 19

NERA

The castle grounds are dark, and the sky sprinkles rain on my skin as I run from the looming building at my back. I remember the moment I first saw the mighty castle that watches over the City of Shifters, like a mother towering over her children. It was beautiful then, but I can't even look at it now.

My bare feet are cold against the wet cobblestones that lead to the city below. I welcome the chill though, after having Reinor's heated lips on mine once again.

He kissed me.

And I ran.

A tear falls down my cheek, mixing with the cold rain. I'm beginning to realize that I do an awful lot of avoiding Reinor when I feel overwhelmed by him. I once thought I could be a strong woman, a warrior who stands up for herself in times of trouble, but I have been walked on my entire life.

"You're a coward," I mumble to myself, slowing my pace as I dip into a long alleyway and hide from the rain beneath a tree.

A male voice startled me from my self-pity. "Oh, well that's not a nice thing to call someone."

I spin toward the sound and my gaze lands on a man in his twenties dressed in rags and looking like this rain is the first bath he has had in years.

He smiles at me through a scruffy beard, all of his crooked teeth flashing in the moonlight. "Who is this coward you speak of?"

I shake my head. "I apologize, sir. I was only talking to myself."

He raises a curious eyebrow at me, stepping close enough for me to see the veins in his skinny arms. "Aw, poor girl. You must be lonely if you're out here talking to yourself."

"I'm not lonely, just crazy I guess." I try to smile back at him, but it falls short. I turn back toward the main road. "I should be heading home."

The man makes a sharp hissing sound, drawing my attention back to him. "Your ears," he says in a whisper. Then his voice rises in a panic. "She's a faerie!"

My eyes widen as I hold my hands up in defense. "No, please. I'm not what you think." I hurry to press my hair down over my ears, but it's no use. The man has already drawn attention.

"A faerie in our city?" A woman says behind me. I turn to find her eyes glowing a dark blue as she looks me up and down, her lip tipped up in a snarl. "What business do you have on our streets in the middle of the night, girl?"

"I was just going for a walk. I'll return home now." I turn toward the main road, but the unwashed man is already blocking my path.

"We can't let you leave now, faerie. You need to be brought to the king."

I shake my head. "Please, just let me go. I mean you no harm, and I won't hurt anyone else either."

"We can't take her to the king," the woman says. I sigh in relief but it's short-lived. "We need to kill her here and now before she can harm our people."

I gasp, and I back away from the pair. "You would kill me just for being Fae? I've done nothing wrong."

The woman sneers at me. "Your kind are filled with dirty magic, from a broken kingdom turned to nothing. You can't be trusted."

I hold up my hands as I continue to back down the alley. "I'll leave the city, then. I'll go to the Fae Wilds and never return."

The woman looks at the man, and they exchange a silent understanding. The man begins to shift in front of me, his body arching as he drops to all fours and fur sprouts along his skin. His jaw elongates into a snout with razor-sharp teeth. He's a wolf shifter, then.

My body shivers from fear, an icy cold seeping into me now from the pouring rain. I don't wait another moment for him to finish shifting. I turn and run as fast as my feet will carry me.

A howl sounds behind me as I turn corner after corner, getting lost in the maze of the city. I don't know how far I've run when something claws at my hair, tugging and scratching.

I scream, ducking my head as I catch sight of the hawk shifter flying above my head. She's large for a bird, the size of a tall child, with sharp talons and shining blue eyes. It's the woman.

She dives at me, but I throw my hands up and nearly scream all over again when I see my skin shining. My magic is coming out, and I have no idea how to wield it for protection.

The hawk backs up anyway, shocked by my glowing hands. She squawks at me, the sound loud in the quiet night.

I start to run once more, but the large wolf has already caught up to me. He slams into my side, knocking me to the wet ground. I hit the stones with my hip and cry out in pain.

The wolf steps over me, his teeth gnashing together as he sniffs the air around me. I throw my glowing hands up to try and stop the inevitable attack he'll bring. I say a prayer to the gods to take pity on me, and a burning light explodes from me, circling the wolf in its heat.

The wolf screams in pain as he falls off of me and thrashes on the ground, rolling in the forming puddles to try and wash my magic from his burning fur.

I watch in horror as the hair melts off the creature's body and he goes limp. The light disappears from him, leaving him burnt and unmoving. *Dead.*

My hands return to normal, all glow fading away as I stand in shock underneath the falling rain.

Another squawk of the hawk draws my eyes up to the sky just as the bird drops toward me, talons extended wide. She is just a foot from me when something massive plucks her body from the air.

A golden dragon.

Reinor's feet crush the hawk, knocking the woman out from the force, and then he softly lays her on the stone ground.

Her body shifts back to the woman she was before, and I can clearly see her chest still rising and falling, calming me for some odd reason. She tried to kill me, and still I don't wish for her death.

I look back up at the golden dragon soaring through the night rain, and just like the day I saw him flying over the city square, I can't take my eyes off of him. I stand and my legs wobble beneath me. My hip aches and my arm bleeds.

Reinor quickly dives down from the sky, his talons outstretched, before he grabs onto my body and swoops back up into the air. All of the breath leaves my lungs in a rush as I'm carried over the city rooftops.

He flies fast back to the massive castle, and he drops down to the ground on the castle steps. I'm released from his strong grasp, and my eyes are glued to the glistening talons of the dragon as Reinor shifts back into his human form.

In moments, he's standing before me with his bare chest slick with rain and black pants covering his legs. Droplets fall from his hair and onto his cheeks, making him look wild and untamed.

Reinor invades my personal space, his eyes still bright and golden as he shouts down at me. "What in the hell were you thinking going into the city like that?"

I draw my chin back in shock. "Excuse me?"

REINOR

"Excuse you? No, I won't!" I'm belligerent, my heart still pounding from the fear of watching Nera getting attacked again.

I swear this woman cannot keep herself out of the eye of monsters. She is like a glowing target, sometimes literally. Tonight, her magic killed a man, and I know that's a hard truth to accept, but I still can't stop yelling at her.

"You run off or shut down every time we are alone together!" I yell. "And you keep putting yourself in harm's way by ignoring the rules I put in place for you!"

Nera steps toward me and slams her hand against my bare chest. Her nightgown is drenched from the rain and her bare feet are scuffed and bleeding, but she is still fighting. "That's the problem here, Reinor! When did we decide that you make the rules and I just blindly follow?" She's the one shouting now. "Yes, you're a prince! I get it!

But, to me, for years you were only a boy and you were my friend!"

She was so much more than a friend to me. "We can still be friends, Nera. I've tried all week to show you that."

She shakes her head. "No, a shifter heir prince and a Fae orphan cannot be anything to one another, except enemies."

I rub my hand along my face, wishing I weren't having this conversation with Nera in a rainstorm. "We're not enemies, and you know what..." I step closer to her, hoping with all hope that she stops running for once. "We aren't friends either. At least...not *just* friends."

Nera's eyebrows raise high as she bends her head back to look up at me. "What does that mean, Reinor? What could we possibly have when you can never leave your title and I can never live amongst people who wish me dead."

"I can renounce my title." I blurt out. "I can run *with* you this time, Nera." My hand rests on her cheek and she sinks into my touch. "My father is still healthy and strong, with many more years to switch his focus onto Calder. Calder will mature and rule."

As I say the words, real hope floods my chest. It's true. I can leave and never look back. I can love Nera freely, as I always dreamed.

Nera blinks rapidly, her shining eyes changing color and settling on a dazzling purple. Could it be the color of happiness, or even love?

"What does purple mean?" I ask her in a whisper, needing to know how she is feeling about my proposal.

Nera smiles softly, a look I crave from her. "Purple means—"

"Sir! Reinor!" Thomin's frantic voice cuts off whatever Nera was saying.

We both turn toward the old man as he runs from within the castle and straight to my side, nearly hyperventilating. "My prince, I must speak with you immediately!"

I release Nera and grip my friend by his shoulders. "Calm down, Thomin. Breathe. What is it?"

Thomin's face is pale as he stares into my eyes. "I am so sorry, my boy. Your father…he was killed on the road to Elf Mountain."

I blink, feeling like I've fallen into a haze of confusion. Can I be hearing him correctly? "I–I don't understand. He's dead?"

Thomin nods slowly. "Reinor, you are now the king of all shifters."

I turn my eyes to Nera, and the purple is now gone from her irises, replaced by a dark gray. I'm a king, and now I know that gray means sorrow because I can feel it in my own heart. We cannot be together.

PART 3
A FAE'S BLOOD

CHAPTER 20

REINOR
Seventeen Years Old

I'm going to see the lost girl again today. I worry about her more than I should, especially because she's one of the Fae. Still, since that day nearly three years ago when I found her half-frozen to death in the Night Woods, I've felt responsible for her.

No, it's more than that. I've felt *connected* to her by something I can only guess is fate.

She has been growing up into a young woman right before my eyes, though I only watch her from a distance, and only for a few minutes every other month. I don't even know her name, but I want only happiness for her.

"Where do you think you're going, boy?" A growling voice stops me in my tracks as I enter the foyer of the castle.

I turn toward the voice and my lips curl up into a smile. "Mr. Minara, you scared me. For an old man, you are quite light on your feet."

His dull blue eyes pierce me with a glare. "Wolf shifters never get old, son. Even us overworked blacksmiths." He winks at me like he always did when I was just a boy. "Are you heading out to stir up trouble with Elex? It'll be sundown soon."

Mr. Minara has always chastised me and Elex for running off at night, but it's the only time the two of us have to train together. My father, King Iredras, forbids me from sword training with my friend. He says my skills will never improve with an amateur. He seems to forget that Elex is the son of the best blacksmith in the kingdom, Mr. Minara, and he has been playing with swords since before he could shift.

I nod to Mr. Minara. "Yes, sir. I'm going to meet up with Elex now."

It's a lie. I have no intention of seeing Elex on this night. I will be spying on a particular young Fae lady at the edge of the city, but nobody knows that.

The old man eyes me suspiciously, his hairy jaw moving from side to side. "You are an awful liar, my Prince. It'll do you some good to work on that if you plan to be king one day."

I stand agape as I shrug at Mr. Minara. "I don't know what you're talking about."

He laughs before turning to walk away from me. "My son is training with the king's army tonight." He raises an eyebrow at me over his shoulder. "So, whatever you're truly heading out for, it better be worth it."

I keep my mouth shut as the man walks away. I won't deny his suspicions, but I won't confirm them either. Luckily, if I know anything, it's that I can trust Mr. Minara with my secrets.

I shake my head and make my way through the front doors of the castle, only to be stopped by a hulking frame with no kindness in his dark eyes. This man isn't like Mr. Minara. He doesn't smile when he sees me, nor does he have my trust.

I square my shoulders and clear my throat as I dip my head at the man. "Good evening, Father."

"Reinor," he speaks my name with no emotion. "I am glad we ran into one another."

My eyebrows raise as I stutter. "Y-you are?" Since when has my father ever been *glad* to see anyone?

My father nods and reaches forward to adjust my lopsided collar. "I have been meaning to speak to you. I think it's time we begin to focus in on your training. No more distractions."

"My training? I don't understand." I can't help but feel lost. My father has no interest in my life on a regular basis. Why now?

He growls and shakes his head in disappointment. "Of course you don't understand, and that's the problem!" He snarls at me. "I am speaking of your training for the day you will take my place as king of the shifters."

"I'm keeping up with my studies, father, as well as strength training in my human form and dragon form. What more can I do?"

My father squares his shoulders and his dark brown eyes glow with a bit of red that matches his dragon. "What more can you do? You can step up and become a man! You can finally take some responsibility for yourself and become the ruler I thought I created when I brought you into this world! I should have known then that you'd fail me one day."

I take a step back, feeling like I was just punched in the gut. "How exactly am I failing you? Everything I do is by your command, to become a king."

He looks me up and down with disgust. "You're weak. Your dragon may be a strong one, but you have a weak heart just like your mother." All of the air leaves my lungs at his words, but he doesn't stop there. "You say everything you do is by my command? I know that you have continued to train with the Minara boy, and I know that you disappear into the city with no word on where you're going. Do you call that my command? Do you call that focus?"

I throw my hands in the air. He doesn't say these things to my younger brother, Calder. Calder can do no wrong in his eyes, but of course he is not heir to the throne. "I'm not meaning to disobey you. I'm doing my best, father!"

He scoffs, his nose scrunched in distaste. "That's the problem, child. Your best just isn't good enough to be worthy of my throne." His eyes fade back to normal as he readjusts my collar once more. "You will have a new schedule come morning, and I expect you to follow it. I will not have a weak heir, do you hear me?"

I clamp my jaw shut tight, my dragon begging to be released. "I understand, Father. I won't disappoint you." I say the words through clenched teeth, but he doesn't seem to care.

My father nods once and then disappears through the castle doors. I growl as I let my dragon burst free and the golden beast launches into the darkening sky.

I won't stop going to see the Fae girl, and I will never stop training with Elex. I can step up my game and prove to my father that I'm not weak like he thinks, but I refuse to ever be like him.

I guide my dragon over the city, to the outskirts where a large manor rests beside the Night Woods. We drop down to the ground at a safe distance from the property, right along the edge of the woods. Hidden from sight, I watch the sun begin to set behind the surrounding mountains.

It's only a few minutes of waiting before I spot the girl bursting from the back door of the home. Her soft cheeks are stained with tears and her bare feet hit the solid ground fast as she runs into the Night Woods all alone.

I watch her wavy black hair sway behind her, and my heart and mind leap into action. Why is she running? Where are her shoes? Why is she crying? Is she hurt?

I call my dragon back until I'm on two feet again with just a pair of black pants hanging on my waist. I run after the girl, struck with worry for this person who has a strange, unbreakable hold of my heart.

Her scent trails behind her, hitting me with the incredible smell of vanilla and lavender. An intoxicating combination that I can almost taste. She stops quickly, falling to her knees once she reaches a clearing in the trees, and even though it's darker in here, the light of the full moon seems to reach this spot more than the others.

I stop at the edge of the clearing, afraid to speak and startle her, but once my bare foot lands on a fallen leaf, she whirls around, lifting to her feet with a gasp. Sad gray eyes lock onto mine, flashing purple as she looks me up and down.

I wonder how her eyes can so easily change color, but it has always been known that the Fae show their emotions in the color of their irises.

Her eyes quickly switch to the blue that I've come to know, and she wipes the tears from her cheeks. "Wh-who are you?"

I clear my throat, trying to find the words. Do I give her my real name? What would she do if she knew I was the prince? "My name is Reinor. I uh…I live out here."

"Oh," she says, surprise in her voice. "I'm Nera."

Nera. Finally, I have the name of the girl that fate brought to me. I can't turn back from her now. "It's nice to meet you, Nera."

CHAPTER 21

NERA
Now

"*I can renounce my title. I can run* with *you this time, Nera.*"

"*Your father...he was killed on the road to Elf Mountain. Reinor, you are now the king of all shifters.*"

I have replayed last night over and over again in my mind on a constant loop. The hope in Reinor's voice when he spoke of running away with me. The look of something like love in his dazzling golden eyes. I believed him. I felt real happiness in that moment, but that happiness was broken when the owl shifter, Thomin, arrived.

Reinor's father, the king of The City of Shifters, has been killed. From one minute to the very next, all of my dreams were killed right along with him. Reinor cannot run away with me now that he is king.

"Dammit!" Reinor's loud voice roars and echoes within the castle, followed by another crash of wood against stone.

This has been going on for a while now. I disappeared into my bedroom after Thomin gave us the news of the king last night. I had no words for Reinor then, or even now. How could I console him when my own heart needed consoling?

After a rough night of tossing and turning, I awoke an hour ago to the sound of glass breaking from across the hall. *Reinor's room.* I nearly ran to him, worried that he was being attacked, or had injured himself. I quickly stopped myself when I heard the loud roar of his dragon followed by a string of curse words from Reinor, and then the maid Lanya asking him to calm down.

He's angry over his father's death, and even though I don't fear him, I don't want to get in the way of his warpath. So, I sit here in a borrowed white slip dress, trying to convince myself to have a little courage and confront the new dragon king.

Gods, I'm lost.

A familiar male voice speaks outside my bedroom, so I hurry over to the door and press my ear to the wood. If I'm not mistaken, it's the swordmaster, Elex, speaking to Reinor.

"Have you enjoyed your tantrum?" Elex asks, his voice low.

Reinor's growl is unmistakable. "Shut the hell up, Elex."

Their feet shift across the floor and then Reinor's door slams shut. I can still hear them, but their voices are now muffled and I can't make out the words.

"Gods," I mutter under my breath. I slowly pull my door open and tip toe out into the now empty hall.

I know I shouldn't be eavesdropping, but I can't bring myself to stop now. I need to know what's going on with Reinor, and this is the easiest way to find out.

Coward? Maybe. Desperate? Definitely.

I lean gently against Reinor's door now, listening closely to the men.

"Lanya wasn't kidding when she told me about your breakdown. It looks great in here, man. I love the remodel," Elex says teasingly.

I don't know much about the guy but he's poking the dragon and I worry for his life.

Just as I thought, Reinor growls again. "I'm pissed! How is my luck such incredible *shit*?" I hear something thud against what I'm guessing is a wall. "All I can do is shift and break things, over and over again. Shift, destroy, shift back, destroy more!" Reinor shouts. "How dare he do this?"

"How dare *he* do *what*? How dare your father go and get killed?" Elex laughs humorlessly. "I'm guessing he had no knowledge of his impending death, Reinor."

Reinor's feet stomp across the room and his voice comes louder. "It is completely his own fault that he got killed! My father was a horrible bastard who made enemies everywhere he went. This wasn't some declaration of war, this was just revenge on one man who deserved it. And just when I think I can see a future for myself where I can actually be happy, his enemies finally get him!"

"Is it really so awful to be king, man? You can do a lot of good for the shifters. Things can change for the better with you as our leader. Don't you see that?"

"I don't want this life! You know that I never have!"

It's silent for a long moment when Elex speaks again. "What would you rather do, then? Run off into the woods with the Fae girl? Disappear with Nera never to return again?"

My heart leaps at his words. Elex must know about our conversation last night, or Reinor has talked about running away with me before. How long has he felt this way?

I wouldn't know, I guess. It's not as if I've ever asked him.

I close my eyes tightly and listen for Reinor's response. "You make it sound so meaningless. Why

127

shouldn't I want to run away and be happy with the girl that I..." His words stop before he can complete that sentence.

The girl that he *what*?

"We can't all get what we want, Reinor. I lost my dad too, and you were there for me. Let me be here for you, alright? I'll stop the sarcasm and actually attempt to comfort you if that helps."

Reinor's low chuckle warms my insides. "Please don't. You'd suck miserably at it."

I smile, grateful that Reinor has such a good friend. But, why do I truly care? As much as I try, I can't hate him for his lies or for the lot that was given to him in life. I just have to accept that I care about him and I don't want him to suffer.

Footsteps move toward the door and I quickly jump out of the way as it swings open. I tuck myself into the shadows of the dark hallway as Elex steps outside and shuts Reinor's door behind him.

Elex pauses in the hall and then turns to me with a cocky grin on his handsome face. "You know, you could go in there and talk to him yourself instead of listening from out here."

I step out of the shadows and try to act cool as he scrutinizes me. "I was just going for a walk."

He shakes his head in disbelief. "Right." His smile falls and his expression turns serious. "Protect his heart, alright? He's a good man, and he will be an incredible king."

I chew on the inside of my cheek and then nod slowly. "I don't have any control over his heart, but I believe you, and I will try my best not to interfere with his destiny."

That grin is back in full force. "Oh, no. By all means, please interfere. I don't think his destiny excludes you in the slightest, Sparky."

I draw my chin back in surprise. "Sparky? That is *not* my name."

He rolls his eyes. "It's a nickname, because you're a sparkly faerie." He wiggles his fingers in the air as if twinkling stars are all around me.

With that, he winks one of his baby-blue eyes and heads off back toward the main part of the castle.

Sparky?

I scoff, but my humor is short-lived. Even though Elex clearly likes to make jokes, something he said tickles my mind, begging for attention.

"I don't think his destiny excludes you in the slightest."

Maybe I do need to find out if Reinor's destiny does *include* me. I rub the dragon pendant that hangs between my breasts. *What do you want from me, destiny?*

And, as always, I get no answer in return.

CHAPTER 22

REINOR

Four days of not speaking to Nera. Four days of preparing for this moment with her just a hall away from me and not getting to hear the sound of her voice. I'd kill to hear her yell at me and call me an ass right about now. That would be better than the silence.

For years, I saw Nera just once every month, and I can't even remember how I survived that distance without losing my mind. Now that I have her within my reach, I ache to go to her, to make her smile if possible.

It's not all her fault that we haven't spoken since the night of her attack in the city. My emotions, particularly my temper, have been up and down since learning of my father's death. I have done nothing to try and communicate with Nera. What would I even say to her now?

If I'm being completely honest with myself, I don't feel sad for losing the only parent I had left. The man who should have cared for me only ever put me down and caused me to grow to hate him. He rarely spoke to me, and when he did, it was almost always harsh words of disappointment.

I might even be glad that my father is gone forever, except that he left me to take over his life, a life that I never wanted.

Today, I am to be crowned king of all shifters in a big display for the citizens. As much as I don't want this responsibility, it's something I will not run away from. There is goodness here in this city, and I intend to protect that goodness. Elex was right when he told me I could do good things.

"Are you ready, my prince?" Thomin stands before me, tilting his head toward the large curtains in front of me that lead to an open balcony.

Once I step out onto that balcony, I will officially become King Iredras, the new dragon king.

I look at Thomin, grateful for his kind eyes. "Is he out there?"

"We couldn't find him. Last I heard he was spending his nights in the pub, but he wasn't there when I went to check." Thomin knows I'm asking about my brother, Calder.

I haven't seen my brother even once since the news of our father, and even now he won't be present for my crowning. It's typical of him, really, but I can't say I'm not disappointed. We are each other's only family now, and he's letting me down.

I nod. "What about Elex, and uh…" I shouldn't even ask if Nera is coming. She wants nothing to do with me.

Thomin smiles gently. "Elex is standing with the guards out front, and Nera…" He glances behind me. "She will be watching from inside the castle with Lanya. We thought it best for her to stay hidden from the citizens."

I turn around and my eyes find Nera instantly. She's standing beside a tall window with her elf maid beside her. Nera is dressed for the special occasion with a tight black dress that flows out from her round hips. Her dark hair is tied up in a loose bun, letting the sides droop to hang over her pointed ears, hiding them from sight.

She looks like a dream standing in the sunlight. Her blue eyes flash to me for a moment and she gives me a soft smile before turning back to the window. And just that smile is enough to encourage me to get moving.

I place my hand on Thomin's shoulder. "I'm ready. Let's do this."

Thomin smiles wide before dipping through the hanging curtain and yelling loud for the crowd to quiet down. All of the voices of the waiting crowd of shifters silence immediately.

"It is a sad day, and one of great joy as well. As you all know, our beloved king who has ruled in this castle for forty long years, is gone from this world, finally reunited with his loving wife, our late queen." I hold in my scoff. There was nothing *beloved* about my father, and if he ends up in whatever graceful afterlife my mother rose to, I would be shocked. "Now, our golden prince and heir to the throne of shifters is here to build us up from our grief and serve this kingdom with strength, power, and devotion to his people!" The crowd hoots and hollers their acceptance. "Welcome, King Reinor Iredras!"

I step through the curtain to an uproar of cheers from the massive crowd of shifters below. All types of shifters from across this city have come to welcome me as their new leader, and for just a moment, my chest fills with pride.

I step to the edge of the balcony and wave to my people as Thomin lifts the ceremonial crown, woven into a peak with silver and gold vines, and places it on my head. The weight of my new role is heavy, but I feel hopeful that I can carry it.

One by one, each person in the crowd shows their devotion to me by shifting into their animal forms. Wolves, foxes, panthers, bears, hawks, and owls all cry out their praise with their animal calls. I hand my crown to Thomin and call my dragon forward.

The beast bursts from me, our golden scales shining in the light of the sun above, and he releases a loud roar of gratitude over the crowd. My dragon spins his head around to peer back at the window beside the balcony, and we lock eyes with Nera who watches on in awe.

My dragon has already claimed her as his, just as much as I have, so he tilts his head to the sky and blows out a long stream of fire, presenting his power for the female he has chosen.

This is the first time my dragon has shown his interest in a mate, but now that he has, I must do everything in my power to make Nera mine.

CHAPTER 23

NERA

I never realized how taxing ruling a kingdom could be. For the past week, Reinor has been in and out of meetings, constantly called into the city on business, and bombarded by the castle staff non-stop. I haven't had so much as a minute to speak with him.

Each day is the same. I wake to the morning sun shining through my window. Lanya brings me breakfast, and then she instructs me to sit on the floor and meditate.

She has explained to me the ins and outs of her elf magic, all of the ways she connects with it. Her hope is to get me to harness my Fae magic and learn to perfect its use. According to Lanya, now that I have released my power, it's dangerous to leave it stagnant.

As I've learned the past few days, she's completely right. The magic inside of me is uncontrollable and dangerous. Anytime I feel overly emotional or frustrated, like when I try to get Reinor's attention and he's dragged away for some important business, I break something. Well, my *magic* breaks something.

I sit in the center of my room, my legs crossed and my eyes closed as I pull at that swirling power within me.

"Come on, magic. Just trickle out slowly."

My fingers tingle with the bits of magic filling them. I take slow, steadying breaths as I work on creating a thin barrier of magic around me, a protection dome of sorts.

This was one of the things Lanya insisted I learned first ever since my attack by the shifters in the city. If I can shield myself, I can run away to safety.

"Just like that," I say, coaxing my magic to cooperate.

I can feel the invisible pieces of magic knitting together around me in an egg-like shape. I release even more power to fill in the gaps of my shield, and a sudden gush of the magic pours out without my permission.

"Woah," I say, attempting to reign it back in.

The power keeps flowing, becoming a river instead of a trickling stream. I can feel myself start to sweat as frustration fills me. I groan against the strain of trying to control the magic, but that only spurs it on more.

"No, no, no!" I shout, and it feels like an explosion of the magic bursts from me like a dam breaking.

My eyes fly open just as the dresser against the wall cracks down the middle and one of the large windows shatters into a million tiny pieces, letting a gust of cold air into the room.

I scream on instinct as glass flies toward me from a sudden whirlwind, cutting my arms and face. Someone grabs me from behind and lifts me to my feet before dragging me out of the bedroom. I spin around to find Reinor panting and looking wide-eyed at me as more magic continues to leak out of me and shift the air around us into a weapon that tears at his clothes.

"Nera, calm down. Take some deep breaths." His hands grip my arms and rub a soothing path up and down my skin, warming me.

I keep my eyes locked onto his as I try to breathe in and out slowly. The force of the power around me starts to die down and I mentally pull it all back into me.

"That's it," Reinor says, breathing deeply with me. "I've got you."

His gentle tone and golden eyes calm me as my body settles back to normal. "I'm sorry," I whisper, looking away from him.

Reinor's fingers grip my chin and he tugs my face back to his. "Hey, it's alright. I'm not hurt."

"But, your window—"

"Can be fixed," he finishes for me. "What about your arms?" He inspects my sliced up skin. "You're hurt."

I shake my head. "Since I've been using my magic, or attempting to at least, I heal much quicker. These will be gone in an hour."

Reinor nods, his thumbs stroking the skin of my cut neck, leaving goosebumps behind. "Is uh…is your magic always like that?"

I look up into his eyes, worried that he's angry with me for continually breaking things in his castle, but all I see is worry on his face. "It's not supposed to be like that, as far as I know. Lanya says I should have had years to hone it, but I never had a teacher." I sigh. "I didn't even know I had magic until that day I healed your brother."

His eyes are locked onto mine and he opens his mouth twice before closing it again, stopping himself from saying something.

"You've been busy," I say, breaking the silence as I step back from his closeness. Just his scent is enough to overwhelm me and make my magic stir all over again.

Reinor runs a hand through his messed up hair from my whirlwind. "Yeah, becoming king so suddenly has really taken its toll. I can hardly find a moment to breathe."

I study his face and can see the exhaustion written all over him. Dark circles rest beneath his eyes and his usual stubble has become more of a beard. Then I look down at his black collared shirt and gasp.

"Oh, Reinor. I'm so sorry."

His shirt has rips all over it, exposing tan skin beneath. His right sleeve is nearly torn all the way off, and a cut stretches across his bicep, though it's already closed and healing.

Reinor chuckles as he follows my gaze to his destroyed clothes. "It's okay. I hated this shirt."

"That doesn't mean it needs to be shredded." I laugh, surprising myself with the sound. It has been so long since I laughed with Reinor.

His gaze falls to my mouth. "Gods, I love that sound."

My heart stutters in my chest and I fall silent, stunned by his admission. "Reinor, I don't know where to go from here."

His eyebrows pinch together on his forehead. "You don't need to go anywhere." He steps closer, his hand rising and then falling with his indecision on whether or not to touch me. "I know we haven't talked lately and I've been busy, but you can stay here with me. I can't run away like we talked about, but I am the king of this castle now. You don't have to feel like a prisoner here." His eyes search my face for an answer I don't have. "Will you stay, Nera?"

I swallow hard, trying to keep my emotions pressed deep down inside of me. Questions flood my mind. Can I really stay here? Would I be a guest of the new king or something more? Would the people here ever truly accept me?

No, they wouldn't.

I shake my head slowly, causing Reinor's face to fall. "I can't stay somewhere I would never be accepted..." I drop my gaze to my feet. "There's nothing for me in the City of Shifters."

Reinor takes a large step back, making me look up to see the hurt on his handsome face. "There's *nothing* here for you?"

I bite down on the inside of my cheek, forcing myself not to reach out for him. It's not fair. "Nothing I can have, Reinor."

I don't wait for his response, and instead I do what I do best. I run.

CHAPTER 24

NERA

I only make it as far as a grassy hill behind the castle before I stop myself. I have no idea where I could go from here. My knowledge of the land is less than nothing, except that the Night Woods stretch out in all directions between kingdoms.

I'd die out there by myself.

I've spent my entire life sheltered, locked away from everything and everyone. With the Cragore's, I was their servant, working on *their* land and in *their* home. Even in the Mortal Lands, my parents kept me home and hidden from the other humans for fear of my identity being exposed.

"Gods, I'm such a child." I hang my head in shame for myself. Who am I to even decline Reinor's offer of a home when I have zero other options?

A voice startles me, drawing a squeal from my throat. "If you're going to be on my training grounds, you'll have to grab a sword." I turn to find Elex standing beneath a shady tree, watching me with a cheek-splitting grin on his face.

He's shirtless and his shoulders are wet with a sheen of sweat. A sword hangs from one hand, and his blonde hair is a total mess.

I look around at the empty green hill. "We're the only two out here. Who are you training with?"

He shrugs. "Myself. I don't need a partner to work on my technique, though one would certainly help." He reaches into a canvas bag hanging from the tree and pulls out a thinner, sheathed sword. "How about it? Care to join?"

"I'm in a dress, and know nothing about fighting." Even as I say the words, I walk toward him and take the sword from his hand. I unsheath the blade and marvel at how good the weapon feels in my hand.

Elex waves a hand at me. "You don't have to know a damned thing about sword fighting. Everyone starts from somewhere." He points to my dress. "And I've seen women fight in dresses before. You can handle it, Sparky."

I roll my eyes. "Ugh, again with the nickname?"

Elex spins his sword in his hand before catching it again in some show-offy way. "You don't like it, then do something about it."

I raise my own sword and step forward with a swing, connecting the blade with his. The vibrating of the swords clashing fills me with a sense of power that I've never known before.

It's not like the spiritual magic that's inside of me. This is purely physical. I may be in desperate need of beating the crap out of something.

Elex lets me attack him with my sword, meeting each of my strikes with his blade. I'm in no way skilled or coordinated in my movements, but Elex says nothing as I continue blow after blow, grunting and growling with pent-up frustration.

I don't stop swinging the sword until I'm out of breath and sweating from the exertion. "Sword fighting is awesome," I say, breathless.

Elex laughs loudly and pats me on my shoulder. "That it is, Sparky. I'm glad we can agree on something." He drops his sword to the ground and sits beneath the tree. "Come sit and complain to me about our new king."

I take a seat on the lush grass and shake my head. "I have no reason to complain about Reinor."

"Nobody goes off on someone with a sword the way you just did unless they've got something weighing on them." He holds his hands out like he knows that I know he's right. "Reinor is my best friend in the world, so I know everything about him, including the details of your relationship with him."

I raise my eyebrows in surprise. "You know about our uh...*past*?"

He nods. "You mean, how once a month Reinor would completely ignore me to run off into the woods to see a *girl*? Yeah, he was a lunatic, but he never smiled more than he did on the days he saw you."

I blush at his statement. Our visits always made me happy too. It was my only escape from the dark reality of my life.

"Well, those days are gone, and Reinor isn't the same person he was then."

Elex scoffs harshly. "He may have a new title and less time on his hands, but he hasn't changed, Sparky. But, since he is too busy to train with me behind the castle like he used to, you can take his place." He winks at me playfully.

My heart aches as the realization dawns on me of how much Elex reminds me of my brother, Benjamin. The teasing, the nicknames, and even that sparkle in his eyes that invites anyone into his world.

"You remind me of someone I once loved. It feels like seeing him again after all these years when I never thought I would." I sigh. "There are a few people I love that I will never see again."

Elex places his hand on mine. The touch is friendly and gentle, no attraction resulting from it as he smiles kindly at me. "You don't have any family here in the city?"

I shake my head. "My family is in the Mortal Lands, that is if they are even still alive. Except for the panther shifter that I consider my sister. She was my only friend on this side of the Night Woods."

Elex nudges my shoulder. "What about Reinor? He's not your friend anymore?"

I scoff without meaning to. "I don't know what Reinor is, Elex."

He shrugs and jumps back to his feet so fast I nearly miss it. He pulls me off the ground and bows before me as if I were some sort of royalty. "Well, my lady. Consider me your new friend then, and *my* friends are Reinor's friends, sooo…" He winks.

I roll my eyes. Yes, he is definitely very much like my brother. "I am one lucky faerie, aren't I?"

"The luckiest."

CHAPTER 25

REINOR

Watching Nera and Elex in the yard the other night made me grateful for my friend, and also gave me the urge to bite his head off at the same time. Seeing how easily he touched her hand or shoulder and she didn't retreat from him. How does that hurt me so badly?

The two of them have met up to train with swords each evening for the past three days. I watch from the castle window that looks into the backyard, all kinds of thoughts flooding my mind. The weather is getting colder by the day and I worry if she's warm enough. I flinch when Elex's sword gets too close to her, and anytime she laughs, my heart clenches with jealousy that he gets to hear that sound and I don't.

I spoke to Elex that first night and nearly let my dragon feast on the wolf shifter, until he told me about their conversation. Nera is lonely and misses her family, and that's what Elex offers her. Someone to connect with.

She needs him more than me right now, and I am grateful to him for convincing her to stick around longer. It doesn't mean I'm going to leave her alone, though. I'm determined to get this woman to feel comfortable here, and I'll do whatever it takes to make that happen.

Two things I know for sure are that she needs people around her that care about her, and I need to find her a proper teacher to help her control her magic.

I knock on Nera's bedroom door and wait patiently for her light footsteps to pad across the floor. She returned from training with Elex nearly an hour ago. I gave her time to bathe and prepare for bed, so this is my chance.

The door swings open and Nera's blue eyes stun me for a moment. She looks breathtaking in a simple white slip nightgown that has thin straps up top, resting on her smooth, tan skin. The gown dips low on her chest and holds tightly to her curving hips, and the bottom rests on her bare feet.

"Reinor?" The question in her voice has me snapping my attention back to her expectant face. *Did she ask me a question?* "What are you doing here?"

"Oh, sorry." I try not to blush like an idiot as I hold out the small stack of papers and ink pen. "Here, I brought these for you."

Nera looks down at the objects in my hands. Her thin eyebrows press together. "What are these for?"

I place the items in one of my hands and reach down to grab her hand in mine. I put the papers and pen into her palm, forcing her to take them from me. "Take these and write to Teyla, if that really is her name." She flashes her gaze up to mine. "Your sister, right? You spoke about her a few times when we would meet up. I'm assuming she wasn't made up?"

Nera shakes her head, a hint of a smile teasing the corner of her lips. "No, Teyla is real. She is the daughter that lived at the manor with me."

"I thought you'd like to tell her where you ended up. I bet she's really worried about you." I know I would be.

Nera sniffles and I notice the little bit of tears gathering in her blue eyes. She stares at the items in her hands and quickly wipes at her eyes. "If I mail a letter to Teyla, her father will intercept it. He shouldn't know that I'm still at the castle."

I have already thought about that possibility. "I'm going to send a messenger directly to the manor. He'll make sure the letter is only read by your sister." I wince, feeling guilty. "I would deliver it personally, but I don't think my people would appreciate their king visiting his subject's homes and murdering them. If I see the panther shifters that hurt you, I may not be able to control myself."

Nera looks into my eyes for a long minute, each second making my heart pound harder in my ears. She bites on her bottom lip before closing the space between us and wrapping her small arms around my neck.

I stop breathing long enough for my chest to grow tight, and then I return her embrace with a long inhale of her sweet scent. She squeezes me tightly and her thick hair tickles my face. My arms circle her small waist completely until my palms are against her ribs on the opposite sides. Nothing can compare to the contentment that I feel at this moment.

"Thank you so much, Reinor." Her voice is low in my ear, causing goosebumps to rise up my back.

"You're welcome, Nera."

She leans away from me and I reluctantly release her from my arms. Her cheeks are flushed red and a small smile graces her pink lips.

"I'm going to write to her now. I'll bring you the letter when I'm finished."

I nod, returning her smile as she closes the large door. I can hear her excited footsteps slap against the floor as she runs across her room, and my grin only grows.

If this is how she reacts when I bring her a few sheets of paper and a pen, I'll bring her a whole damn tree and barrel of ink.

CHAPTER 26

NERA

My eyes are closed as I sit beneath the cloudy sky. Winter is just around the corner, and the air is turning cold. I chose the castle gardens as my meditation spot today, hoping that the feeling of nature surrounding me will calm my nerves.

I shiver against the cool breeze that brushes across my skin and immediately wish I would've brought a coat out here with me. I ignore the chill and place my hands on my folded legs. Flowers that have survived the changing seasons surround me, filling my nose with their sweet scent.

I take a deep breath and reach within myself for that glowing magic. Here goes another attempt at wrangling in this wild power. It has been a rough week up in my bedroom creating whirlwinds of destruction and then leaving to spar with Elex in the yard.

My body is sore from learning my way around a sword, and practicing the many maneuvers that Elex insists I must know. Reinor's busy schedule as king has made me his replacement for Elex's torture. Okay, it's not *that* bad.

I've truly loved Elex's company and the strength I feel while fighting. It has given me something to look forward to, as well as waiting patiently for any sort of response from Teyla since she got my letter. It has only been two days since I gave the letter to Reinor for delivery, but I feel anxious for her response.

I steady my breathing again and focus on my power. Drawing the trickling energy into my limbs warms my body against the harsh weather, causing me to sigh.

"Thank you, magic," I whisper to the power. I'll try anything to make this magic respond well to my command, even speak kindly to it.

Tendrils of power flow from my skin, connecting with the dirt beneath me and the air surrounding me. I can feel the tendrils grow and extend like they always do, much too quickly.

"Come on, we can do this," I say, breathing deeply.

It only continues to float away, reaching out to the flowers and plants around me. The magic latches onto the living things and smothers them in its strength.

I struggle against the intensity of my magic, sweating now on this cold day. My head becomes fuzzy as I fight to pull the magic back within me.

"Not again," I grind out. My breathing becomes ragged and too quick for my liking. The fuzziness in my mind intensifies until I can feel the world turning beneath me, and everything fades to total darkness.

I open my eyes to night all around me. I can wiggle my legs and arms, but I cannot control them enough to stand or even roll over.

The taste on my tongue is bitter, and I can feel myself grimace at it. I turn my head from side to side in confusion, seeing forest all around me for as far as I can see.

Where am I?

I look back up at the dark canopy of trees above, just as a man leans over me and into my view.

"Hush now, baby girl. The ward is complete so you'll be safe here."

His words make no sense to me, but they also comfort me in some way. I can't speak or respond in any way to the man, so I merely watch him as his familiar blue eyes shift to gray and cloud with tears.

He is Fae, just like me, and we even look remarkably similar. His skin is creamy and looks soft like mine has always been. His hair is dark brown and hangs in waves to his neck, his pointed ears poking out the sides. And even his lips curve deeply at the top just like mine.

Could I be looking at a blood family member of mine? But why can't I speak or move?

"I will love you always, my darling girl. Nobody can harm you under my protection. Only those with good intentions may know you are here, and that is how your rescuers will find you. Do not fear."

The man wipes at his eyes before leaning in to kiss me on my head. He takes a long look at me once more before running off through the trees and disappearing.

All I can hear are the cries of an infant as I lie there unable to do anything but watch the leaves above. Footsteps startle me until another face enters my line of sight.

This face I know well, and my heart soars at the sight of him so young and safe. I haven't seen him in years. It's my Pa, the human one who rescued me in the Night Woods as a baby.

He bends before me and I'm lifted easily into his strong arms as he speaks soft words to me. "I've got you, child. You're safe now. Let's get you home, alright?"

I gasp as my body lurches up and the sun blinds me from where it peeks out from behind thick clouds. I shield my eyes and swallow gulps of air as I double over.

I'm back in the castle gardens, beneath the cloudy sky. I don't understand the memory I just had or if it was simply a dream.

But when did I fall asleep?

I look around to find the flowers and greenery all burnt to ash in a wide circle around my body. The ground smokes from the heat still radiating from it, but my body isn't so much as scratched.

"What just happened?" I ask the empty air around me.

I must have blacked out from overexerting myself and dreamt of some other place and time. The dream felt so real, like I had truly lived those moments in the woods…and maybe I did.

I was told at a young age that my Pa found me abandoned in the woods as a baby. If that was some sort of memory from that day, the other man had to have been my biological father.

He just left me there with promises of safety. But why did he leave?

My mind races with the new memory, playing the man's face over and over again when a familiar voice calls out my name.

"Nera!" Teyla's excited squeal has me jumping to my feet and searching the castle grounds for her.

She turns the corner of the large castle and runs at panther speed toward me, her smile wide and her long black hair flying in the wind behind her. "There you are, sis!"

I gape at her, my brain taking way too long to catch up with my eyes. "Tey?"

She launches her tall, thin body into my arms and hugs me tightly to her chest. Teyla is taller than I am, just like most other shifters, but I can easily reach my arms around her neck.

"Are you really here?" I ask, still stunned.

She giggles and steps away from me with a nod, until she spots the burnt garden around me. "Uh, what happened here?"

I shake my head, gripping my sister's hands in mine. "It's a *long* story."

CHAPTER 27

NERA

"Are you sure you're okay after just blacking out like that? Maybe you need a healer to look over you." Teyla's concerns over my well-being bring a smile to my face.

I shake my head as I sit with her on a stone bench that rests at the entrance of the royal gardens. I've sat here before to marvel at the beauty of the flowers and stone pathways, though now some of that beauty has been destroyed by my magic.

"I'm okay, Tey. I shouldn't have told you all that right after seeing you for the first time in weeks."

She turns toward me with stunned gray eyes. "You mean, you shouldn't have told me that you have magic powers that can burn a garden down and make you pass out and dream about the Fae father you never knew but who left you in the forbidden woods as an infant, where you were found by a human male who adopted you into his family and raised you as his own?"

She releases a long breath and I can't stop the harsh laugh that shoots out of me. "In a nutshell, yes. That's a lot of info to dump on someone. The whole Fae father abandonment thing is even new to *me*." My smile falls. "It may have not even been real."

Teyla sighs and takes my hands in hers. "I am so glad you told me all of it, Nera. Do you know how closed off you have been since the day you were dropped at our doorstep? It's an honor to know the real you *finally*."

A huge pressure lifts from my chest. I squeeze her hands. "So, I can't believe you're really here. All crazy magic drama aside, you must have gotten my letter."

Her face lights up with excitement. "Yes, I got your letter, and I can't even tell you how relieved I was to know you were alive and well." Her smile turns into a wry grin. "And the messenger certainly wasn't bad to look at either."

My eyebrows shoot up. "Who was the messenger? Reinor said he wouldn't deliver the letter himself."

"Oh, you mean Reinor the secret lover from the woods who turned out to be our crowned prince turned king?" She shoves my leg with a knowing look. "No, his highness did not deliver my letter. A gorgeous wolf shifter with dreamy blue eyes and the sexiest smile in existence was *my* messenger."

Only one man with that description comes to mind. "Are you talking about Elex?"

"Yeah! That's his name!" She sighs with a dreamy look on her face. "Elex, *yum*."

I hold my hands up between us. "Wait, what about your fiancé? Shouldn't you be daydreaming about Mathis?"

Her nose scrunches up in disgust and she lets out a little growl of anger. "Mathis is dead to me, and it's lucky for him that he's not just dead period."

I tilt my head to the side, waiting for some sort of explanation, so she continues. "The day my father took you away, that day of trial, I thought for sure you'd be killed. I shifted and fought my parent's guards. I was able to escape them, and the first place I went was to the castle in the hopes of stopping your execution." She shakes her head. "My father was already on his way back when I ran into him. I asked him to tell me what happened and he said you were gone. I asked if you'd been killed, but he refused to answer. He only said I would never see you again and disturbing the king for information on a faerie would get me locked away."

"Teyla," I say, taking her hand. "I'm so sorry."

She clicks her tongue. "Don't you dare be sorry. It's my parents who should be sorry." She takes a shaky breath, real anger in her gray eyes. "Anyways, I went to Mathis after that. I opened up to him about you and asked him to marry me that day so I could leave my parents. I didn't want to return to the manor after what they had done. Well, Mathis told me that I should be glad to be rid of a Fae slave and that my father did the right thing!" She growls again, her eyes flashing silver. "Ooh, I could have ripped his throat out right there. I told him how much you meant to me, and he still sided with that monster!"

I rub my hands along her arms, trying to calm her rising panther. Panther shifters don't normally lose their tempers so easily, but Teyla has a heart of gold and is loyal to a fault.

"You didn't have to break your engagement for me, Tey. He could have cared for you and given you a good life." Guilt sits heavy in my heart for her.

Teyla snorts and rolls her eyes. "Oh, please. That man was as boring as they come. I want what you have with Reinor. I want passionate kisses in the woods and true, *deep* feelings. *Attraction* at least."

My cheeks blush with heat. "I don't know how much truth is in that, Tey."

She smiles softly now, her anger gone. "Nera, I heard you talk about him that night before you were taken away. I also read it in your letter. Why hide it?"

I sigh and throw my head back in a groan. "Ugh, I mean, from the beginning there were so many lies. Then, he captured me like some lowly prisoner, and *now* he is the king of a people that will never accept me as even a citizen in their city. How could I possibly be with him? Be his *queen*?" A long silence stretches between us. "And then there's the wild magic inside of me that I can't come even close to controlling."

Teyla shrugs. "Is there any way to learn to control your Fae magic? That elf woman you wrote about. Can she not teach you?"

I shake my head. "Lanya told me that my magic is much stronger than anything she knows. It's hopeless."

"It's not hopeless." The masculine voice has Teyla and I spinning around on the bench where Reinor approaches us with Elex at his side.

Reinor speaks again. "I have a plan."

I stand from the stone seat and cross my arms, warming myself from the cold breeze. Teyla hurries and dips down into a proper bow. "My king," she says, her eyes cast down.

My eyebrows rise and I shake my head in exasperation. "Is this how I am supposed to be greeting you?" I ask Reinor.

He smiles wide as Elex snickers behind him. "I may drop dead in shock if you were to ever bow to me, Nera." His eyes seem to sparkle as he stares deep into mine before turning to Teyla. "Please stand, Teyla. I am nothing other than your friend here."

She rises and her eyes find Elex as she blushes. "Thank you for inviting me here." She smiles at Reinor. "Both of you. It was incredible to get to sit down and talk with my sister again."

"Thank *you* for accepting my invitation," Reinor says. "You don't have any problem traveling with us?"

Teyla shakes her head. "Nothing is keeping me in the city. I'm in this for Nera all the way."

"Wait, traveling?" I look between the three of them who all seem totally on board. "I'm guessing this would be a part of your so-called plan to help with my magic?"

Reinor steps toward me. "I've seen how you struggle with this new magic, and I spoke to Lanya about it. She can't help you the way you need it. You need a Fae trainer, and the only way we'll find one of those is by traveling to the Fae Wilds." He looks back at Teyla. "When Elex delivered your letter to Teyla, he also delivered an invitation from me for her to join us on our journey. We leave in the morning."

I chew on the inside of my cheek. "You're going to just leave your kingdom behind? You only just became king."

He shrugs. "Thomin is on top of it, and I am not about to send you away without me looking out for you." He points to the others. "And those two also." His eyes lock with mine. "Your magic will only grow and could eventually overwhelm you. It's this or risk hurting yourself and others."

I sigh, but a new excitement lights within me. "Okay, but if the trip becomes dangerous, I won't risk any of your lives." I look at Teyla and Elex who both smile warmly back at me. "We leave tomorrow, then."

CHAPTER 28

REINOR

"You're certain this is wise, my king?" Thomin eyes me with expectancy, but I won't give in.

I nod. "She needs me, Thomin. I know my duty is to my people, but a kingdom cannot function without a level-headed king. If I send her away to do this on her own, I will be a useless ruler."

Thomin raises one eyebrow. "You are leaving the city in the hands of your brother. How is that for a useless ruler?"

I laugh at his words and cause a bright smile to light his face. "Calder will have you to guide him. The city will survive while I'm away. Once we can find a teacher for Nera who will return with us, we will be back."

"And what if no Fae will come?"

Stubborn old man.

I sigh. "I have faith that we'll find one. Don't you believe in me?"

Thomin places a hand on my shoulder. "I do, and I always will."

"Please look after Calder. You know him as well as I do, but don't let him sink into nothingness, alright?"

Since our father's death, Calder has been a ghost in the castle. He appears half-alive and mostly drunk, but disappears before I can speak to him. I worry for his health and his future.

The door to the den opens up and Calder steps inside, looking from Thomin to me. I step back in surprise. "Calder, you're here."

He nods and I realize how clear his eyes are. He's not drunk. "I uh...I was told by Elex that you're leaving. I thought I should speak with you."

Thomin clears his throat and moves toward the door. "I will go prepare a bag for your trip, sire."

Thomin leaves the two of us alone, and Calder fiddles with his hands nervously. I wait for him to speak, and when he does, I nearly fall over in shock.

"I'm sorry," he says softly, his brown eyes casting up to mine. "I'm sorry for the way I treated your girl, and I'm sorry for not being here for you when Father died. I've been...lost."

I stand agape for a long time, my eyes looking into his. "I'm sorry too," I finally say.

Calder scoffs. "What do you have to be sorry for?"

I run my fingers through my hair. "Honestly, a lot of things. I don't think I've been a great big brother to you since we were young. I never really appreciated our lives here. I wanted out, which meant wanting to leave you behind. I was selfish."

"But you didn't actually leave, Reinor." Calder shakes his head. "How can you be sorry for wanting something if you never even got it?"

I shrug. "Because even though I didn't leave physically, I was gone mentally and emotionally from you. Just like Father."

Calder chuckles humorlessly. "Father was an ass and you know it. You might have been distant, but you're nothing like him." He shoves his hands in his pockets. "I've been drunk nightly since he passed, and it's not because I am sad for losing him. It's because I am sad for the wasted life I've spent as his son. I want...*more*."

My eyebrows pinch together. "You want to be king?"

He laughs loudly and shakes his head. "Oh, hell no!" He throws his hands in the air. "I just want to live. I want true responsibility and maybe even some freedom, but I don't want to leave. I want to take part in my life finally."

I sigh and a small smile lifts my lips. "Well, how about you start by looking after things while I'm gone? When I come home we can spend some time together, find something you'd like to pursue for the future."

Calder nods and I can see his shoulders rise like a brick was lifted off of each one. "I'd really like that, bro. And I'll do whatever it takes to make things right with Nera, alright?"

I nod and for the first time in years, I take my brother into my arms in a real hug.

NERA

The large canyon rests before us, a hulking mountain split in two, pointing our way toward our destination. Cold wind blows from the canyon, causing goosebumps to rise along my skin.

Reinor, Teyla, and Elex stand beside me. Each of us has a pack on our backs and heavy boots on our feet. The morning sun is barely rising above the mountain and adrenaline pumps freely through my veins.

"You guys ready to get in there?" Elex points to the line of towering trees that fill the bottom of the canyon.

The Night Woods

The massive castle stands behind us, blocking us from the City of Shifters as we prepare to dip into what they know as the forbidden woods.

Teyla claps her hands together in front of her. "I'm absolutely ready for some adventure." She raises an eyebrow at Elex. "Think you can keep up, Pup?"

His eyes narrow at my friend as he rubs his own hands together. "Oh, you have no idea what I'm capable of, *Kitten*."

I look up at Reinor by my side and he raises his eyebrows with a knowing grin on his face. He sees what I see in our friends. Something is building between those two.

"You sure you're ready to take on the Night Woods with me once again?" Reinor asks, his eyes especially gold in the light of the morning sun.

I take in a deep breath of fresh air. "Gods, I don't think I've ever been more ready. It's like returning home, even though the Fae Wilds never really were my home."

Reinor shrugs. "They were meant to be your home, though."

"Yeah, maybe." I'm not so sure where my home was meant to be.

Reinor takes the first step forward, his boot crossing into the dark woods while we follow behind him.

After a few steps, he turns to me with a big smile. "So, did you ever hear the story about how the Fae Wilds got their name? It used to be called *Faedom*, the kingdom of the Fae, until their big fall."

I shake my head, suddenly intrigued. "No, I've never heard of it."

Reinor hikes his bag higher on his back before eyeing me with excitement. "Well, then. Settle in for one hell of a story."

PART 4
A FAE TORN

CHAPTER 29

REINOR
Twelve Years Old

"Settle down, Calder. You must learn the history of our people." My mother tugs my younger brother by his shirt sleeve and forces him to sit beside her on the circular rug at the center of the den.

I shake my head at Calder as he grumbles and throws his head back. "The faeries *aren't* our people, though. Why do I need to know about them?"

My mother's gentle smile stretches the pink skin of her cheeks. "Oh, my dear boy. Our world is much larger than you think. The four kingdoms may remain separate, but we are all one world, which means we are all *one* people."

"That's not how Father sees it," I say, shaking my head. According to my father, the king of shifters, all other kingdoms are our enemy unless proven otherwise.

Mother scoffs and rolls her chocolate-colored eyes. "Your father is a powerful king, but he does not have compassion in his heart." She leans forward and rests her palm against my chest. "Do not be a compassionless king, my son. Promise me."

I square my shoulders as my eyebrows scrunch together. "Why does it even matter what sort of king I am?"

"It matters a great deal, Reinor. A kingdom can always grow and improve, but without a good king, it can crumble just as well." Her eyes pierce through me for a long moment, letting her words sink in, before she smiles and clears her throat. "Now, both of you listen."

I nod at the same time as Calder groans, but we both remain silent as our mother begins telling the history of the Fae Wilds.

Her melodic voice fills the den. "Years ago, when I was just a child, the Fae Wilds had another name. It was known as *Faedom*, a thriving kingdom of faeries. I visited with my parents, and you wouldn't believe the beauty of the Fae kingdom then. It seemed as if the treetops touched the clouds. Long stretches of wooden bridges hung between their branches, creating floating streets above the ground. Walking those bridges was incredible, like flying without my dragon wings." She sighs at the memory. "The royal family at that time were in constant fear of some of the Fae living on the outskirts of their towns and within the Night Woods. These Fae weren't like the others. These ones were raised in the wild, in camps, and they were closer to animals than faerie."

"Animals, like shifters?" I ask, intrigued.

My mother shakes her head, her dark hair swaying against her neck. "No, dear. They didn't change from man to animal, as we do. They were wild day and night, and *vicious*. These Fae lived off of blood instead of food. In fact, many people called them the *Blood Fae*." My nose scrunches up in disgust as Calder's eyes widen in fear. I have no problem with eating meat, but to drink blood is something else entirely.

Mother continues. "The Blood Fae stayed out of the main towns in Faedom for a long time, but they began to attack the locals more regularly. One night while I was visiting Faedom, there was an attack just two blocks from where I slept. Six Fae were killed and drained of blood."

Calder gasps, and I lean in further. "Did you see any? Did you come back home after?"

Mother shakes her head. "I never saw them, but yes, we left immediately after hearing about the attack. Once we returned to our city, we received news that the Blood Fae rose up against the royal family and ambushed their castle. The king and queen were murdered, and their two children disappeared. Very quickly after that, the kingdom fell." Mother's eyes show real sadness for the Fae people. "The Blood Fae were once thought to be mindless animals, but they planned it all. They completely took over the capitol city and ran most of the Fae out into the wilderness, and into hiding. Over the years, as I grew up and married your father, Faedom became known as the Fae Wilds, no longer a true kingdom."

I sit still, staring wide-eyed at my mother as I imagine such a horrible place with blood-sucking creatures. "But, what happened to the children of the king and queen? If they survived, they could take back the throne."

My mother shrugs her shoulders. "Nobody knows where they ended up, but many believe they went into hiding. Hopefully, Faedom will someday be rebuilt."

"Do you think that's possible?" I ask.

My mother grins back at me, her pink lips stretching wide. "Anything is possible, my son. *Always* remember that."

CHAPTER 30

NERA
Now

"You're serious? There are creatures out there that drink blood?"

"There are far worse things than even the Blood Fae in these woods, Nera. Always be on guard."

Reinor's words echo in my dreams, causing fear to rouse me from sleep. I slowly sit up and blink in the dark night until my eyes come into focus. My rapid breathing settles as I take in my surroundings, and I let out a sigh of relief.

I'm safe.

Two days ago, I left the City of Shifters on a journey toward the Fae Wilds, or *Faedom* as it was once called. The dragon king, Reinor, and my two friends, Teyla and Elex came with me in the hopes that we can find a faerie to help me control my magic. Trying to tame the wild power inside of me has been difficult, and dangerous.

We've made camp twice now in the dark of the Night Woods, surrounded by thick forest, and no sign of daylight.

With my Fae sight, I can see well enough in the dark, but not nearly as well as the shifters. The sounds of insects and small animals skittering around echo throughout the woods, but no real dangers have come upon us yet.

I look to my right where my best friend, and sister, is curled up like a cat on the cold ground. Thanks to her panther side, the soft sound of purring vibrates from her chest as her long black hair hangs across her face. To my left rests a flickering campfire that barely warms me enough for comfort. All of my companions are shifters who run naturally warm, so they don't need the fire like I do.

Across the fire, I can see Elex, the wolf shifter-slash-Sword Master for the shifter army. He is sprawled out, deep in sleep with his blonde hair sticking up in all directions. Unlike my purring friend, he sleeps silently.

I cast my eyes to the empty spot beside Elex, and my heart leaps in alarm. *Reinor should be there.*

I jump to my feet and scan the dark woods surrounding us. "Reinor," I hiss, trying not to yell and wake my friends. The cracking of a twig sounds behind me, so I whirl around, a scream getting trapped in my throat before any noise can escape.

I heave a sigh of relief as Reinor's golden-brown eyes lock onto mine from where he stands at the edge of camp. "Nera, are you alright?"

"Gods, Reinor." I place a hand on my chest as I whisper. "I woke up and saw that you were gone. I was worried."

His plump lips lift up at the corners as he steps quietly toward me. "You were worried…about *me*?"

I cross my arms across my chest, the chilly air causing me to shiver. "We may have had our arguments, but I don't wish you dead, you know?"

"I'm glad. I wasn't so sure." He grins, and my insides melt a little despite the weather. "I was just scanning the perimeter to make sure our camp is safe for the night. You can never be too safe out here."

I study his handsome face and notice the slight hollowness around his eyes. "Have you slept at all since we left home?"

His eyebrows raise high. "Do you consider the castle your home, Nera?"

I roll my eyes and rub my arms for warmth. "Y—no…I mean…You know what I mean, Reinor." I groan in frustration. "Have you slept or not?"

He shakes his head and runs a large hand through his thick brown hair, but his smile never fades. "No, I haven't slept yet."

"Reinor…" I start to chastise him, but he takes a long step toward me and swiftly pulls the thick fur coat off of his back. He drapes the coat over my shoulders and clasps the front closed with his fist, tugging me close to his chest in the same movement.

I gasp as his hot breath hits my cheeks and his golden eyes peer darkly down at me, his smile falling. "How could I sleep when I know you're vulnerable out here, Nera?" His voice is the softest whisper. "Just let me protect you, because I don't know any other way to stay sane."

"I don't need your protection," I say, my voice quivering from his nearness.

A gentle rumble leaves his deep chest as his eyes narrow. "No, you don't *need* my protection, but *I need* your safety." He takes a step back, but his eyes don't leave mine. "Do you understand?"

I nod, swallowing a large lump in my throat. "Okay."

He points to the large coat hanging off of me. "Are you warmer now?"

"Yes, thank you." I scan his body, realizing he's completely fine in just black pants and a short-sleeved brown shirt that hugs each of his muscles. "If you are warm like that in this cold weather, why even bring the fur coat?"

"Honestly?" He shrugs. "It's sort of a comfort thing, I guess. Dragon shifters run hot, so I rarely feel cold, but it's nice to have the fur against my skin."

I pet the soft coat and snuggle deeper into it, Reinor's delicious scent flooding me. I suppress a moan as I nod in understanding. All of my years living with the Cragore family, I was never given a coat nearly as warm as this one, even when I was forced to work out in the yard in the winter time. That's the luxury of being a king, I suppose.

"Why are you awake at this hour, Nera?" Reinor asks, stepping around me to stoke the fire.

I settle back on the ground and Reinor sits beside me, shoulder-to-shoulder. I try to ignore the pull I have toward him as I focus on the flickering orange flames. "I had a nightmare about Blood Fae drinking from my birth father, after he left me in the Night Woods all those years ago."

"Yikes," Reinor shakes his head. "So, you're pretty certain the man from your vision is your father, then?"

I nod. "It was real. I can't imagine my mind making up that moment. It was an actual memory, I'm completely sure of it."

I told Reinor and Elex about the vision I had of a man leaving me in the woods outside the Mortal Lands when I was an infant. He put a ward around me so that only those with good intentions could find me, and my adoptive father did find me that day.

Teyla is sure that my birth father wouldn't have left me unless I was in immediate danger, and he must have come back for me but been unable to find me after my human dad took me away.

Elex believes my birth father must have died that day, or else he would have found me eventually. I don't know what I believe. If that man is still alive today, he would probably be living in the Fae Wilds now.

Reinor nudges my arm. "Maybe we'll find him when we cross the border a day from now. We're close."

I shake my head. "It's not possible. I'm just not that lucky."

Reinor's eyes find mine again and he smiles gently. "You know what my mom used to tell me, Nera?" I shake my head. I know nothing about the late queen. "She'd say 'anything is possible', and I believe that now."

"What makes you believe that?"

He blinks and his eyes turn back to the fire. "I found you, didn't I? I'd call that luck…on my end at least."

My cheeks heat with a new warmth as his words sink into me. Maybe I am lucky, at least a little bit.

CHAPTER 31

NERA

"Are you sure you don't want to sleep?" Teyla curls up beside me like she has been each night.

I look off into the trees where Reinor and Elex walked off a few minutes ago, and I shake my head. "Reinor has been awake for three days now. I can't sleep knowing he's patrolling all night." I shiver at the tingling feel of power under my skin. "Either way, I'm not sure I can sleep with that border so close to us."

I nod toward the wall of magic that practically pulses beyond the trees. I would only need to walk thirty yards to touch it.

We walked all day long, barely resting long enough to drink and eat, but we have finally arrived at the border between the Night Woods and the Fae Wilds. When Reinor told me the border was a literal wall of magic, I never imagined this.

The wall stretches around the entire Fae Wilds, completely protecting the Fae from the woods surrounding them. I imagine the Fae have more enemies within their borders than they do outside, though. Especially with the blood-sucking Fae that control their capitol.

Since reaching the wall an hour ago, I have had a constant pull in my chest toward the pulsing magic. It's like my body knows that once I touch that magic, I will be fully charged with raw power. It's a craving like I've never known before.

I close my eyes and shake my head, attempting to rid myself of that feeling. "Do you feel drawn to the border, Tey?"

She turns onto her back, not even fazed by the cold dirt beneath her. "I don't. If anything, I feel a danger radiating from the magic that I don't want to touch." Her nose scrunches up in disgust. "Do you think it'll hurt to step through?"

I shrug. "I wish I knew. Reinor said the Fae once needed to open sections of the border to allow visitors through. I guess this will be a test for us."

"Ugh," she groans, closing her eyes with a long yawn. "I hate tests."

I laugh softly as Teyla easily drifts off into sleep within moments. This is going to be a long night.

NERA

I lie awake, my entire body buzzing from the magic of the Fae border so near. The Night Woods are dark, as usual, but being so close to the edge gives me a rare peek through the tall canopy and at the millions of stars sparkling high above.

I can't help but hope that once we enter the Fae Wilds tomorrow, I may finally see my father. I know there have to be many Fae within those borders, and many dangers as well, but hope still flutters deep inside of my tired heart.

If I find my father, I can really learn about who I was meant to be. Maybe I can learn who I am once and for all. I've never had a purpose before. The feeling of being lost, or trapped, is all I am familiar with.

I blink up at the stars and sigh into the night just as a small whimpering sound floats to my ears. I jerk up from the ground and scan the sleeping bodies around the fire. Reinor is leaning against the trunk of a tree, sword by his side. His eyes are closed and a soft rumbling snore leaves his lips. Finally, he sleeps.

The whimper comes again, but it's not from my friends. I listen closely to the sounds of the woods. Suddenly, a long whine whistles from nearby, causing me to pinpoint the direction.

I walk slowly toward the sound, but I stop in my tracks when I realize where the cries are coming from.

The long border of magic surrounding the Fae Wilds stretches in front of me, so close that I could touch it. The wall isn't solid, just a floating mist filled with strong magic. I reach my hand forward and stroke the mist. A tingling fills my fingertips and rises up my arm, making me shiver.

"Wow," I whisper, feeling suddenly alert.

The whining from across the border is close, so I peer through the wall and my eyes land on an animal like nothing I have seen before.

It's covered in thick black fur that floats around it like smoke. The animal resembles a fox, but much larger, with more than one long tail behind it. At least four tails spread out behind the animal as it writhes against the forest floor and cries out in pain.

I spot something metal clamped tightly around the animal's front leg, and inky-black blood pours from the poor creature. It pulls against the metal clamp and then cries out before dropping to its side.

Without thinking clearly, I run forward, only thoughts of helping the animal in my mind. As if I command it, the magical mist parts for me, creating a door in the wall for me to move through.

I pause for a moment, stunned by how the magic moves for me, and then I continue forward. I am within just a few feet of the large black creature when it startles and jumps back to its feet. The movement makes the animal cry out again, and more blood drips from the wound on its leg.

"Shhh." I try to calm the creature as I whisper to it. "I'm here to help you." I hold my hands up to show that I'm not armed.

The animal's large black eyes narrow at me, and it bares long, sharp teeth as it snarls. The sound is menacing, but I can see pain behind the creature's anger.

"Please, let me help you out of that trap," I whisper. "You can run free the moment I release you." I wait as the animal slowly calms and its tall, pointed ears droop down once more. "Trust me," I add.

I step forward and then sink slowly to my knees, my eyes searching the metal device for a way to pry it from the animal. My fingers touch the cold metal and the creature jerks back from me.

I pause and study its black fur for a moment, afraid to move. It's clear that the creature is female, so I smile up at her as I begin to feel around the metal clamp once more.

"You're a girl, like me." I stare up into her eyes. Black blood drips around my fingers as I find the base of the clamp. "You're beautiful, but I have no idea what you are."

She doesn't take her eyes from mine until I squeeze the bottom of the metal trap as hard as I can, opening up the metal prongs wide enough for the creature to pull her leg out.

She jumps back and I release the trap, letting it snap shut. I toss it to the side and stand back up, my hands in front of me as I brace for an attack from the animal.

She backs up a ways, stepping tenderly on her hurt foot, and her eyes pierce me as she stands to her full height. She's huge for a fox, her head rising higher than my own, and her clawed paws as long as my feet, every part of her completely black. There's no doubt in my mind that she could kill me in an instant.

I slowly begin to back away from her, my heart pounding. "There you go, girl. I hope you heal fast and don't get yourself stuck in any more traps." I smile weakly, pointing my thumb behind me. "I better get back to my friends."

Her head tilts to the side as she listens to me with perked-up ears, and then she begins to growl low and menacingly. The tiny hairs across my body stand straight at the terrifying sound.

I take another step back, ready to turn and run, but the creature's head whips to the side just as something dark and impossibly fast slams into her side.

The wounded animal drops, unconscious, but the new threat whirls on me with needle-like fangs and hollow holes where eyes should be. This creature isn't an animal, it's made purely of gray skin and black shadow. It leans forward on long, clawed, human-like hands and then it charges forward.

A scream rips from my throat, just as my magic bursts from my chest and blinds me.

CHAPTER 32

REINOR

A horrifying scream tears me from sleep, and I'm frozen on the ground before reality comes crashing in. I'm in the Night Woods with Elex, Teyla, and...

Nera.

I scramble to my feet and look around our small camp. *Nera isn't here.* A chill prickles my skin and my heart gallops in my chest as I realize that scream came from her.

"Nera!" I yell into the night, but I'm already caught onto her scent as my dragon surges forward to help with my senses. I don't allow the shift to come in case I need to help Nera in my current form.

She's not far away, but when I reach the border to the Fae Wilds, I pause. The border is torn open, a doorway for anyone or anything to pass through.

I step carefully through the opening, knowing that the magic could rip me apart if I touch the mist. On the other side, Nera is standing with her arms stretched out in front of her, her body shaking with power that she can't control.

Magic floats all around her, creating a hardened barrier where a Dark Elf uses its long nails to claw against the magic. Its body is made of shadow and a thin, gray skin. Parts of it fade in and out as it constantly shifts from shadow to creature and back, still unable to penetrate Nera's magic.

The Dark Elves are nothing like the Elves of the mountain. They are creatures of nightmare that feast on anything with a beating heart. Right now, this monster has his hollow eyes locked on Nera.

I growl low in my chest as I let just my talons stretch from my fingertips and my golden scales layer my body in armor.

The Dark Elf spins and hisses as its sights set on me. I don't hesitate to charge the monster, using my dragon strength to tackle it to the ground. I stab my long talons into the thing's chest, but it fades into shadow in an instant. I fall through the creature and onto the ground.

"Shit!" I yell, turning just in time for the Dark Elf to lunge at me now from behind. These things can move through shadow, and right now, the entire forest is cloaked in darkness.

It screeches at me as its nails rake across the scales on my right arm. My scales act like armor, so the Elf's strike doesn't pierce me.

I rock back, twisting my body and shooting my talons up towards the creature. It staggers back, caught off guard with a new gash across its gray abdomen.

A blur of motion appears at the corner of my eye, so I turn and find Elex's wolf, and Teyla in a battle of their own with a second Dark Elf. According to legend, the Dark Elves rarely travel in pairs, unless they are mated.

If these two are mated, they will stop at nothing to defend their mate and go into an unstoppable frenzy when their mate is killed. That means they both need to die or one of us will die instead.

"Do whatever it takes to kill that thing," I shout, getting Elex's attention.

His wolf eyes turn to me and he growls before spinning and locking his jaw in the leg of his Elf.

The Dark Elf in front of me has regained its composure, and its entire body tries to shift to shadow. The gaping wound on its abdomen tears open more as the Elf attempts to shift, and it screams out in pain.

I take that moment to attack again. I turn and pull the dagger from the sheath on the back of my pants. I stab the dagger through the Dark Elf's chest just as it flickers back into a solid form.

The monster screams, its voice echoing all around us as it sinks to its knees and crumbles to the cold ground.

A feminine cry has me spinning on my heels, and I find Nera falling to the dirt, her shield gone, and her magic swirling uncontrollably around her. All eyes turn to her, and at the same moment, the other Dark Elf spots its mate dead in the dirt behind me.

The gray, nightmarish creature screams just as its mate had, and its hollowed out eyes widen until the dark shadows take up its entire face. In a matter of seconds, the creature evades an attack from Teyla's sword, slipping into shadow and reappearing directly behind Nera who is in a battle with her own magic.

"No!" I yell, crouching to run toward the monster. I know in my heart that I'll be too late, though.

The Dark Elf solidifies, its shadowed hands rising to strike my Nera while she remains unaware. But, before it can lower its claws to Nera, a black mass slams into the Elf's side.

A large black Shadow Kitsune tackles the Dark Elf to the ground and then opens her large mouth to bite down on the Elf's neck. The Elf's screech is cut off by a killing crack of its neck, and then the Kitsune drops it from her jaws.

Nera's magic slows as her eyes stare wide at the dark beast in front of her. "Thank you," she whispers, her breathing heavy and tears staining her pink cheeks.

I run forward, meeting Elex—now shifted back—and Teyla. The three of us guard Nera, ready to fight the newest threat to our girl. The Shadow Kitsune growls at us, her nine tails rising and her black eyes narrowing.

"Wait!" Nera pushes between me and Elex, but I grab her around the waist before she can move toward the Kitsune.

"Don't go toward it, Nera!" I shout.

She whirls on me, her blue eyes shifting to red and back. "She *saved* me, Reinor. She's not going to hurt me."

"We don't know that she was trying to save you," Teyla says from where she stands beside Elex.

Nera turns her back on the glaring Kitsune, and she looks at each of us one at a time. "I know she saved me because I saved her first. She was caught in a metal trap until I helped her out of it."

I stare agape at this crazy girl in front of me, and my words pour out before my brain can think better of them. "Are you out of your damn mind?" I grab her by the wrist before she can make another stupid decision. "You left the safety of our camp to cross the Fae border *alone* and walked right into a Dark Elf trap! Don't you know that the Dark Elves capture shadow animals to use as bait for their meals?" I groan, anger and fear for Nera mixing into belligerence. "You made yourself a damn meal, Nera, and risked us all!"

Her eyes shift to a bright red as she glares back at me. She rips her arm out of my grasp. "How would I know any of that, Reinor? *You* are the one who brought me on this trip! I know nothing about these woods or the creatures that live here!" She steps back, the angry Kitsune at her back now. "All I saw was a wounded animal that needed help, so I helped her."

Gods, I'm an idiot.

"Nera—" I start, but she stops me with a hand held up between us.

"Save the lecture, your highness." She reaches for Teyla's hand and pulls her sister to her side before locking eyes with me again. "I'm sorry if I caused you all to be in danger, but I'm out of my element here and you knew it the moment we stepped into the Night Woods."

Teyla stares wide-eyed at the Kitsune as it steps to Nera's other side, and Nera gently pats the beast's neck. "Come on girls. Let's go find a spot to rest for the night while the boys gather firewood." Nera drags Teyla behind her as she walks away from us with the giant fox staying close by her side.

I turn to Elex and rub a hand along my face, feeling like I just fought in a war. "What the hell just happened?"

My friend's hand falls on my shoulder. "I think Nera just told the shifter king to gather firewood while she walked off to bed with her pet Shadow Kitsune." I raise my eyebrows at him, and he smiles back at me. "Some trip, huh?"

CHAPTER 33

NERA

I'm walking ahead of the group with no idea where I'm going, but I can't face them after last night. I'm angry, and scared, and honestly...embarrassed.

I *should* know more about the magical creatures in this world. I was so sheltered in my human home for twelve years, with the ideas that magic and mythical beasts were only made-up stories.

Then, I was dropped at the Cragore home, suddenly immersed in the world of shifters, but I was no more than a servant meant to clean, cook, and remain silent.

I know Reinor didn't say I was naive, but he implied as much, and he was right.

I need to know more.

Something bumps against my shoulder, pulling me from my thoughts. I turn to find the Shadow Kitsune walking beside me, her long black legs moving slowly to keep pace with my short legs.

We've been walking for hours through the Fae Wilds since waking up this morning. The sun is high in the sky, and the freezing cold from the Night Woods is gone, replaced entirely by a sticky heat that has me practically panting.

Reinor is sure we'll find signs of other Fae soon, but it has been quiet. The Kitsune, that I've learned is a large, nine-tailed fox made of shadow and capable of disappearing in one spot and appearing in another with something called "shadow stepping", has been by my side off and on throughout the day.

Elex grumbles behind me. "Oh, great. The beast is back."

I turn to glare at him just as Teyla smacks him in the arm. "If she is a beast, then what are you, *Pup*?"

He folds his long arms over his chest, blue eyes narrowed on my sister. "I am a wolf shifter, *Kitten*. That *thing* is made of literal shadow. It's…disturbing."

Reinor sighs, drawing my attention to him where he walks a ways back from me. "She's just an animal," he says, his golden eyes not meeting mine. "And it looks like she has imprinted on Nera, so we're stuck with her."

"Imprinted?" I ask, confused once again.

Reinor looks at me finally as he nods. "It means she has claimed you as her master. I've heard that the shadow animals will imprint on powerful people and become loyal to only them until the day they die. Looks like this one has chosen you."

My eyes widen as I stare into the black eyes of the Kitsune. "You've chosen me?" Her large, furry head nods, and my eyebrows shoot up even higher. "Do you realize that I'm not powerful? Are you sure you don't want to imprint on Reinor? He's the king of the shifters."

Teyla steps up to me where I've stalled on the path through the woods. Her arm goes around my shoulder. "Sis, you are incredibly powerful. It's the whole reason we're on this adventure to find you a teacher." She smiles and her high cheekbones nearly touch her gray eyes. "Should we give the big girl a name?"

I shrug and look from Tey, to Elex, and then to Reinor. None of them have any suggestions, so I say the first name that pops into my mind.

I smile up at the shadow fox. "How do you like the name Smoke?" She tilts her head to the side and then licks her lips. "When I first saw your fur, I thought it looked like smoke billowing from you. Even though it turned out to be shadows that circled you, could I still call you Smoke?"

Her head nods at me once again, and my smile broadens. "Thank you, Smoke." I reach out and stroke her soft neck.

"Nice to meet you, Smoke," Elex says. He steps beside Teyla and I with a welcoming nod to my new "pet". "Do you like to swim?"

Smoke just stares back at him, so I ask the question for her. "What does swimming have to do with anything?"

Elex points to our right, and we all look at the same time. A sparkling lake rests through the trees with an incredible waterfall cascading from the rocks above it.

"Wow!" Teyla gasps. She looks around at each of our faces. "Last one there is a rotten egg!" And then she takes off at a supernatural pace toward the water.

Shadow runs after her, all nine tails wagging in excitement, and Elex shifts in seconds and takes off at wolf speed.

I grin as I watch the three of them dive into the crystal clear water at the same time. Reinor steps in front of my view and holds a hand out for me to take. "Shall we?"

I blush as I place my hand in his. Before I can speak, Reinor tugs me to his body and throws me over his broad shoulder. I squeal and kick my legs, but it's too late. Reinor jumps, and we both sink into the cool water.

I break through the surface and pull in a deep breath of air. "King Reinor Iredras!" I shout as he launches out of the water with a big splash in my face.

He laughs loudly, causing every cell in my body to heat up. He reaches for me, grabbing onto my waist and pulling me close. "Before you get all angry, come with me."

"Fine." I let him drag me through the small lake toward the rushing falls, trying to ignore the sudden pounding of my heart.

A low growl comes from behind me, causing Reinor and I to both spin around. Smoke is standing neck-deep in the water with her black eyes piercing into Reinor as she snarls at him.

Reinor sighs. "She will be safe with me, Smoke. Do not worry."

I add a nod to the Kitsune, and it seems to be enough to reassure her.

Reinor pulls me through the cold waterfall and turns me in his arms so I'm forced to look up at him. "I don't know if I like you having such a fierce protector that isn't me." He growls like Smoke had, and it makes me smile.

"I'm grateful to have her…just like I'm grateful to have you." I chew on the inside of my cheek, suddenly nervous. "I do have you, right?"

His golden brown eyes glow softly in the shadows of the waterfall. "That you do, Nera. You had me from the moment I found you all those years ago." He brushes his wet thumb across my cheek. "And you will always have me."

I swallow a lump in my throat as I stare up into those eyes that I know so well. "I'm sorry, Reinor. For causing trouble last night…I never meant to—"

His thumb moves over my lips, stopping my apology. "I'm the one who is sorry for getting angry. You were right to help Smoke. You have a kind heart, Nera, and it's just one of the reasons I've loved you for so long."

I blink up at him, my chest aching with emotion. "You really love me? Even though we lied to one another? Even if I will never belong in your world?"

His large hands cup the sides of my neck as he presses his chest to mine. "I do. Unquestionably." He searches my gaze with his. "What about you? Do you love me in spite of all of that?"

I don't even have to think about it. "I do. Unquestionably."

Reinor's hand slips into my wet hair while his other one lifts me by the waist so we are eye level. His glowing eyes drop to my lips as he speaks with pain in his deep voice. "I kissed you once without your consent, Nera. Please don't let me make a fool of myself again."

My lips tug up into a sly smile at the corners just before I crash my mouth to his. I throw my arms around his neck and finally allow myself to get lost in this craving.

Reinor's chest rumbles against mine as his lips, hungry and eager, move against mine. His hands swing around my back and he lifts me up, my legs slipping around his waist beneath the water.

His tongue peeks out between his lips to stroke mine, and I meet his movements with my own, sinking into a new passion that I didn't know was possible. I've never known where I truly belong, but this place feels more right than any others. *Reinor* feels right.

Reinor kisses me until I'm gasping for breath, and Elex's voice interrupts my heated thoughts. "Uh, guys…" Reinor spins toward his friend with narrowed eyes, but he doesn't release me. "I am honestly sorry to interrupt your…heart-to-heart, but we sorta have company."

CHAPTER 34

REINOR

Elex's words sink in, officially pulling my mind back to the task at hand, and not solely on the feel and taste of Nera.
Though I really liked getting lost in her.
I lick my swollen lips and separate myself from Nera, but I still take her hand in mine. I'm not ready to part from her, especially after she told me that she loves me.
"What do you mean by *company*?" I ask, following Elex through the rushing waterfall and back into the warm sunshine.
My question is answered though when I see the many Fae warriors circling the shoreline of the lake. On instinct, I tug Nera behind my back and grip the dagger sheathed at my waist.
Be ready to shift, I prepare my dragon in my mind as scales slowly stretch across my skin.
The Shadow Kitsune, Smoke, is growling as she stands before us in the water, facing the Fae threat. Teyla is standing beside Smoke with her hands up, ready to fight if necessary.

One of the Fae, a tall male with bright yellow wings at his back, steps to the edge of the water. His eyes scan the group of us still standing in the center of the shallow lake. "We are not going to harm you...unless you make us."

"Who are you?" I ask, still shielding Nera.

The Fae dips his head, long blonde hair falling over his shoulder. "I do not owe you my name, but I'll give it anyway, to encourage trust. I am Shieran, Major General to the Fae army." He waves a hand in my direction. "And you are?"

I square my shoulders, wishing I was out of this water and level with the General. "I am King Iredras of the shifters, and these are my companions."

Shieran raises his eyebrows in surprise. "The shifter king in our land? To what do we owe the pleasure?"

I open my mouth to respond, but Nera shoves her way past me and Elex to stand beside her Kitsune. "We came looking for a Fae teacher to help me understand and control my magic. My name is Nera." She tucks her wet hair behind her head to reveal her pointed ears.

Shieran shakes his head, looking confused. "A Fae girl traveling with the shifter king, two shifters, and a Shadow Kitsune. In all my years, I've never seen such a sight." He looks back at me. "You are helping this woman. *And* you allow her to speak for you?"

I can't help my small smile as I shrug. "I do not *allow* her to do anything. If she wishes it, it is hers."

Nera smiles back at me as the General chuckles. "Well, you certainly have me intrigued. I would like to take you to our king. Will you travel with us?"

"As your prisoners?" I ask, feeling my dragon stir beneath my skin.

Shieran shakes his head. "As a guest to the Fae king." He glances at Smoke. "The Kitsune cannot come with."

Smoke growls, the sound menacing. Nera lays a hand on the animal's back. "Can you find me wherever I go,

Smoke?" The beast nods. "Then, go rest somewhere safe. I will call for you if I need you."

Smoke hesitates, but she nods once and then walks to the shadow of a nearby tree and disappears, leaving the Fae stunned as they watch her go.

"Okay then," Shieran says. "Let's make haste before nightfall. You won't want to meet the Blood Fae that feed in this area...trust me."

REINOR

Our small group follows behind the Fae General, Shieran, through the Wilds. The woods are dense with incredibly high treetops and an eerie calm that is constant as we travel.

Nera walks close beside me, her fingers occasionally brushing against mine. Every touch is insanely distracting and all I want is to take her away from all of these people.

Even with the memory of Nera's lips on mine threatening to make me take her on a detour, I'm still capable of keeping up with the quick feet of the Fae.

I smell the fresh air, and am surprised by the lack of mixed scents. "I assumed the Fae Wilds would have more life in them. Where are all of the inhabitants?"

Shieran looks over his shoulder with a dark look in his eyes, changing the color from blue to gray in the same way Nera's eyes change. "Since the fall of the Fae kingdom, the Blood Fae have become unhinged. They hunt more often than before, meaning they kill more as well. Many creatures have deserted our lands in fear."

I begin to fear for the safety of my own group as the sun begins to set over the treetops. We've made good progress, but I have no idea how much further we have to go. Then, as I am ready to ask, we start to hear the first rumblings of life up ahead.

The trees open up to reveal a rocky mountainside. The mountain reaches high into the darkening sky, and stretches far to the sides of us. Still, I hear people, but I don't see anyone.

"Do we need to climb this?" Nera stares wide-eyed at the hulking mountain before us.

Shieran's men gather beside the large stone wall at the base of a cliff, and the General waves us toward him.

"We don't climb the mountain." He touches the slab of rock and closes his eyes. Glowing magic leaks from his palm and onto the rock, creating a tall and wide circle of light. The light fades, leaving behind a hole in the mountainside that wasn't there before. Shieran smiles proudly at us. "We go *into* the mountain."

Elex chuckles behind me, clapping his hands together slowly. "Damn. I'm officially impressed."

"Uh," Teyla squeaks nervously. "You want us to go into a cave beneath a massive mountain? What happens when the mountain decides to cave-in?"

Elex raises his hands in a "who cares" manner. "If it starts to cave in, run really fast, Kitten. I'm sure you'll outrun it." He winks, causing Teyla to growl at him.

"It won't cave-in," Shieran interrupts. "The cave was created by magic. No natural disaster can destroy it."

Teyla steps up to the General and loops her arm through his. "Well, let's head in then, shall we?"

Elex grumbles under his breath as he stomps ahead into the mountain, and the rest of us follow closely behind.

"What's his problem?" Teyla asks in a whisper, looking back at me and Nera.

I point to where her arm is linked with Shieran's. "I'd guess jealousy."

Shieran looks down at his arm and then up at the back of Elex's head. "Oh, a lover's quarrel, then?" He pulls his arm free of the panther shifter. "I better not interfere."

"No, it's not " Tcyla starts to protest, but Nera interrupts.

"Why don't we go meet this Fae king that was thought to be dead, eh? Sounds like a good chance to get some help."

We certainly do need help.

CHAPTER 35

NERA

I'm in awe of the interior of the mountain. This isn't just a cave, it's a palace. Everywhere I look—plush carpeted rugs, framed artwork, and smooth, polished stone walls that stretch in all directions in long hallways.

Other Fae come and go through carved doorways, many women and children eyeing our small group curiously, and even fearfully. It seems as though women are not common as soldiers here, like the men in our party. It's not like that with the humans.

Reinor touches the polished wall to our left. "What was this place created for?"

"It is a safe house, built after the Blood Fae ran us from our kingdom." Shieran stops before us to speak to one of his men, his tall frame lean but strong.

I haven't seen men like these Fae before. They have elegant faces with smooth, perfect skin. Each of them wears their hair long over pointed ears, and they have wings on their backs. I never knew the Fae were meant to have wings.

I quietly reach behind me, my fingers grazing the skin of my upper back. Reinor's eyebrows raise in question before he gently takes my hand in his.

"What is it, Nera?" His voice is quiet, only for me to hear.

I look around, suddenly embarrassed, but nobody is paying attention to me. "They all have wings. Why don't I?"

Reinor's lips form an "o" as he seems to realize this for the first time. "I honestly haven't thought much of it. Shall we ask?"

I nod and step toward Shieran, grabbing his attention. "General Shieran, would you mind answering a question for me?" He smiles and nods. "I was raised by humans, so I know nothing of my own kind. Could you explain why I don't have any wings like you all?"

"Ah," Shieran smiles kindly. "I understand your concern, but you have no need to worry. How old are you?"

"I am nineteen."

He nods. "Our children reach maturity at eighteen, and only then do they fully realize their magic and release their wings." He looks me up and down, but not in an uncomfortable way. "Have you drawn your magic out? You said you need a teacher to help you control it."

I twirl my fingers together nervously. "An Elf woman helped me to use my magic for the first time only weeks ago. I have been unable to use it without losing control."

"Then you should be ready to release your wings. The first time can be painful and quite damaging, so it is best to have someone coach you through it." He waves a hand for us to follow him. "My king can help you, if you'll let him."

Reinor grasps my hand in his, our fingers intertwining. I smile up at him, wishing I could kiss him right at this moment. He winks a golden eye at me, and pulls me forward to follow the Fae through the long tunnel hallway.

REINOR

We head down the passageway, lined with candle-lit torches. Elex trails directly behind Teyla, his eyes not straying from her. My friend is a smart ass most of the time around Teyla, making an idiot of himself, but I know he's hiding deeper feelings.

I understand exactly how he feels.

The hall ends at a wide archway that leads into a massive room with wooden tables spread around the space.

A few Fae sit at the tables, some eating dinner while others play card games. The only indication of where the Fae king sits is that his table is larger than the rest. I spot him immediately, noticing how he carries himself with more confidence than the others.

His blue eyes turn on our group and he stands quickly. "General Shieran, I'm glad you've returned safely." He looks from me to Nera, noticing our hands clasped together, before eyeing Elex and Teyla with curiosity. "What do we have here?"

Shieran dips his head to the king. "King Airden Faven, I present King Reinor Iredras of the shifters, and his traveling companions."

"Your highness," I dip my head in respect.

He reaches forward to shake my hand. "King Reinor, I was sorry to hear of the death of your father." Alarm bells ring in my head, but before I can make an accusation, the king stops me. "I assure you, the Fae had no part in his murder. We believed it to be grudging elves."

I nod. "As do we. My father wasn't loved by many."

"I am still sorry, though. In truth, I am not the official king of Faedom." He glares playfully at the general. "Shieran and his men mislabel me."

"Then who is the king?" Nera asks.

He smiles at Nera with interest in his eyes, causing my dragon to stir with jealousy. "My uncle was the last king, but he was killed by the Blood Fae when I was just a boy. His sister, my mother, was killed just days before him, leaving only me behind." His smile falls as his eyes turn gray with sadness. "The royals don't last long in these lands once the Blood Fae catch word of them."

I shake my head, not understanding. "But if you are the only royal still living, you are the rightful king, are you not?" I don't know a lot about Fae customs, but I know this much.

Airden sighs. "My uncle was married and had a child just before his death. That child is our true ruler."

"Where is it?" Nera asks, her eyes threatening to shift color with her intrigue. "The child. Where are they now?"

Airden waves at the large table behind him. "Come and dine with me. This is quite a long story."

CHAPTER 36

NERA

Most of the lingering Fae have left the large dining hall by the time we receive our food. Multiple platters of various meats, cheeses, bread rolls and desserts are placed along the table for Shieran and his men, and the four of our group to enjoy.

I continually notice Airden's blue gaze lingering on me as I fill my plate and my belly with the delicious meal. Though he stares, I don't feel threatened or even uncomfortable because of it.

I can feel Reinor's tension beside me, though, so I lay a hand on his thigh beneath the table, hoping to reassure him.

Reinor's eyes turn to me and I give him a small smile. "Thank you," I whisper.

His head tilts to the side. "What are you thanking me for?"

"For bringing me here." I look around at the cavern. "I think I'll find real help here, and I have you to thank for that."

His plump lips rise at the corners, causing his strong jaw to widen. "You're welcome, then, my Nera."

My heart flutters and a red blush stains my cheeks, but Airden clears his throat before I can launch myself at the dragon king.

"I hope you have all had your fill and enjoyed the food we have to offer."

"We have," Elex says from the other side of Teyla who sits to my left.

Teyla nods. "It was incredible. Thank you."

"Yes," I add. "Thank you for your kindness."

Airden grins back at me, looking very much his age with that youthful grin. The Fae king is handsome, tan, with long black hair that's tied behind his neck. His eyes hold a sadness that asks for sympathy, but his muscular body shows real power.

"Now, I will tell you the story of my people." He leans back in his chair, his eyes meeting each of ours one pair at a time. I barely notice the soldiers filtering out of the room, probably returning to their families for the night. All that's left behind are the four of us, Airden, and his General, Shieran.

He continues. "The fall of Faedom began with my grandparents. They ruled this kingdom with strength and an abundance of love. I'm sure you've heard the stories, so you don't need me repeating them, but I'll give you the gist. When my mother was a young princess in the castle in our capitol city, the Blood Fae rose up and attacked her home. Her parents were killed, but my mother and her older brother escaped with a group of castle guards."

He pauses, taking a heavy breath. "The guards took the Prince and Princess to a safe house outside the city, where more Fae gathered and made a plan to hide. They traveled far from the city while the Blood Fae continued to go on a rampage, killing all who didn't escape in time. My mother and uncle were ushered to this mountain here. The Fae survivors used magic to burrow into the mountain and create this place." Airden waves around us. "The Prince and Princess spent their remaining youthful years here, awaiting their adulthood when they planned to take back their kingdom. My mother fell in love with a soldier, resulting in me. Together, they raised me."

    Airden sighs. "Well, my mother raised me at least. My father died in battle with the Blood Fae when I was an infant. At that same time, my uncle took his place as king and began making his plans for redemption. I was just three years old when the king fell for a Fae woman. They married and prepared to attack the castle once and for all. My uncle's wife, the queen, became pregnant, and my mother fell ill soon after. The queen was nearly due to have her baby when my mother passed from her illness while the queen was out gathering herbs to help with her fever. The Blood Fae took the queen from the woods that very night."

    I gasp, my hand flying to my heart. The idea of a pregnant woman in the hands of those monsters makes me sick to my stomach, and taken the same night Airden lost his only parent. *Gods.*

    Airden's story doesn't stop, though. "My uncle lost his mind. He and just a handful of his guards went after the queen, but only one guard returned. He told us that they found the queen drained of blood and left for dead, but they were miraculously able to save the baby. The king took the child, and ran as Blood Fae began to attack them."

    Airden pauses, but I am on the edge of my seat now. "What happened to the king and the baby?" I ask, my voice trembling with emotion.

    His sad gray eyes look into mine for a long moment before he simply shrugs. "Nobody knows. We never saw him alive again."

CHAPTER 37

NERA

"What?" Teyla asks in a high voice. "That's it? The king and his heir were just lost forever?"

Airden nods, his eyes constantly looking toward the doorway behind him as he speaks. "Almost. The king's body was found not far from here, drained of blood, but the baby has been lost ever since. My uncle's advisors raised me and trained me to become their new king, but the royal magic never came to me."

I feel a sudden flurry of emotions—sorrow, grief, rage—all crashing into me for the number of losses Airden has endured. How could this have happened? An entire kingdom falling in a single attack?

Reinor speaks beside me, asking the very question in my own mind. "What do you mean by 'the royal magic'?"

"It's exactly as it sounds. The Fae rulers from thousands of years ago were given the magic of their people as sacrifice when the royals demanded it for repentance. This practice ended a long time ago, but the mass amount of magic that had built up was still passed from generation to generation in the royal family. Only the eldest child of the king and queen received the magic, though, and if that child died, the magic transferred to the next rightful heir. My uncle had the royal magic in him, and when he died, that magic went to his child."

I lean my elbows onto the table. "And if the magic never went to you, that means the child is still living out there somewhere."

Airden nods and I catch something like pride in his bright eyes. "Exactly."

"So what happens now?" I ask, my curiosity piqued.

Airden opens his mouth to speak, but two more Fae enter the room from the door behind him. All of us look up to see the newcomers, and every muscle of my body freezes as I spot the woman approaching me.

Her dazzling blue eyes that were once green smile back at me, and her bouncy, gray curls are exactly as I remember them. New wrinkles shape her red lips and the corners of her eyes, but this is the same woman I met on that horrible night nearly eight years ago.

"Madame Karista?" I gasp out her name, my throat feeling tight now.

The elderly woman nods, and her smile brings me back to what feels like a lifetime ago. "Hello again, Nera Larc. You have grown to be as beautiful as I always imagined."

I blink fast as I attempt to figure out what alternate reality I've landed in. Reinor grips my chin and turns me to face him. "Who is this, Nera? How do you know this woman?"

I shake my head in disbelief. "She was a fortune-teller in the Mortal Lands. I went to see her at a fair with my family on the same night I was forced to flee into the Night Woods." I look into Reinor's worried eyes. "You found me a few days after that, Reinor."

Reinor launches to his feet with a growl ripping from his throat as he stares down Madame Karista. "You did that to her, didn't you? You had something to do with her nearly dying in those woods!"

The woman raises her hands. "I saw Nera in that fair and not once more until this very moment. I did nothing to her, young king."

I stand too, laying a hand on Reinor's arm. "She warned me that I'd be attacked by the humans. She knew it would happen, but she wasn't the cause." I turn to Madame Karista. "You're Fae?"

She nods. "Yes, I am, dear. I couldn't tell you then, but I wanted to, terribly."

"Did you know we'd end up here? Meeting again?"

She nods, but her face is sad. "I knew everything, darling. I knew Reinor would find you, and I knew you would endure all of those years hurt by those terrible panther shifters." She glances at Teyla. "No offense, hon."

Teyla shakes her head. "None taken. They suck."

I shake my head, upset now. "Why didn't you tell me? Why didn't you help me if you knew all of that?"

Madame Karista steps forward, stopping across the table from me. "I had to let you discover your own fate, Nera. If I disrupted your process, you never would have found your fated mate."

"What?" Reinor asks, his voice almost a whisper.

"Yes," the woman smiles at him. "You and Nera are fated for one another, but you couldn't fully feel it with her large amounts of Fae magic overpowering the bond."

"It's true then," Airden says loudly, his eyes flicking from me to Madame Karista. "You're sure? It's her?"

She nods to Airden, and something squeezes tightly in my chest as pieces begin to fall into place. "What are you both talking about?" They stay quiet, so I shout at them, officially losing my calm. "Tell me!"

Reinor's large hand rests against the small of my back as Madame Karista locks eyes with me. "Nera, your birth father was the last Fae king. You are the lost princess, the rightful queen of the Fae that holds the royal magic needed to save our kingdom."

All at once, the air in my lungs escapes and I fall backward, only to be captured in strong arms. Reinor holds me close to his chest as he asks questions I can't hear from where I've sunken into myself. This can't be real.

I look over at Airden, my *cousin*, and his eyes watch me with worry and a hope that I can't possibly fuel. "Nera, you have a choice. Do you understand that?"

I take a breath, but the air feels like sandpaper in my throat. "What choice could I possibly have?"

He leans across the table so that I'm forced to focus solely on him. "Now that you have returned to us, we can save our people. You can become the queen we have needed for so long…or you can transfer your magic to me." He pauses, his eyes reflecting the green in mine that only comes when I'm most lost. "The fate of this kingdom is in your hands, Nera. What do you wish to do?"

PART 5

A FAE CROWNED

CHAPTER 38

NERA
Twelve Years Old

I stare forward at my reflection in the cracked glass of my vanity mirror. Ma stands behind me, her delicate fingers combing through my thick tangle of hair as she creates new styles atop my head.

She twirls the dark hair and pins it back so that my pointed ears are open to the world. Well, the private world of my bedroom.

I sigh, feeling truly beautiful for the first time as I notice the way my lips are plumper than they used to be. My blue eyes don't look too big for my face anymore, and my torso has finally started matching up with the length of my legs.

If only these ears were round like Ma's.

I meet my mother's gaze in the mirror. "Why do I have to be different, Ma? Why can't I be like you, Benjamin, and Pa?"

Her eyebrows press together on her forehead as she stares back at me. "Darling, you *are* like us. You tease in the same ways I do. You have your father's genius mind.

And you're incredibly stubborn, just like your brother." She laughs. "Why do you think I get so frustrated when the two of you team up against me and Pa? You're a tough team to say no to."

I smile at that. Ben and I fight a lot, but we really are good at working together. Ma is kind, but she's wrong about me.

I shake my head. "That's not what I mean, Ma. I wish I wasn't a faerie. I wish I could be human."

Ma spins me around in my chair and glares down at me with fierce brown eyes. "My beautiful Nera. Do you think it matters one bit what type of creature you are?"

My eyebrows raise high. "Of course it matters. It's why humans live here, and magical creatures live across the Night Woods."

She folds her arms across her chest, more stubborn than she realizes. "Look at me. All of me." She gestures from her brown hair to her oval-shaped face. She points to her arms and fingers, and down to her bare feet against the wooden floor. "You and I have more of the same features than we do different ones. We have hair, eyes, ears, lips, shoulders, bellybuttons, curved hips, ten fingers, and ten toes. We eat and digest our food in the same ways. We breathe air into our lungs. We speak and listen just like one another." Her hands grasp mine. "I do not care whether you are a human, a faerie, an ape, or even a dragon. You are *my* daughter, with a heart that is capable of so much love, for me, Benjamin, Pa, and some day the person who will become your everything."

I nod, understanding what she means. It certainly doesn't matter to me what she is. I still love her the same. And her love for Pa is one I hope to one day be capable of having, but I'm not so certain it will ever come for me.

"Do you think someone will ever love me for what I am? That they can ignore the point of my ears and the magic in my eyes?"

Ma smiles wide. "I have no doubt about it whatsoever. But promise me something, my girl." I nod and she continues. "Promise me that when that true, forever kind of love finds you, that you will accept it and fight for it with all that you have. If they love you for *who* you are, not *what* you are, hold onto them forever."

I bite on the inside of my cheek, unsure if someone like that exists in my world. "I promise, Ma."

She leans forward and kisses me on my cheek before quickly wiping her lipstick stain off my skin. She reaches up and pulls the clip from my hair, letting it fall over my ears, hiding them from the other humans.

"Now, let's grab the boys and head to the fair. I'm ready for a fun night out with the three loves of my life." She winks and drags me from my bedroom and through our cozy house.

Maybe it really doesn't matter what I am on the outside. As long as I have family in my life, I am home.

CHAPTER 39

REINOR

Nera's small hand is warm in mine as we follow the Fae General through the wide cave halls. It's well into nighttime, but within the mountain, we wouldn't know the difference.

My mind is racing with the overflow of information that has been given to me, Nera, Elex, and Teyla. This isn't what we expected when the four of us began our journey into the Fae Wilds just less than four days ago.

Speaking with Airden Faven, the chosen king of the Fae people, has stunned our group to silence this evening. The Fae woman, Karista, has just told Nera that the man who left her in the Night Woods nineteen years ago, her father, was the Fae King.

Nera is a lost princess.

Not only that, but the woman I have spent years falling in love with is actually my fated mate. Fated mate bonds have *never* been known to occur between different species, but here we are.

My mate is the rightful queen of the fallen kingdom of Faedom. She has the ancient magic of her family inside of her, uncontrollable and powerful, and now we must spend the night in the center of a mountain surrounded by the evil Blood Fae who want nothing more than to eradicate the royals from this entire land.

Gods, help us.

Help *her.*

General Shieran halts outside two heavy wooden doors that have been shaped to fit perfectly in carved stone arches within the cave. He waves a hand toward the closed doors.

"Here we are. These two rooms have been prepared for the four of you. Please disperse as you wish." He dips his blonde head toward each of us, but his blue eyes linger on Nera, shifting to a bright yellow as he bows lower. "If you wish to have better arrangements, I am more than happy to accommodate you, our lost queen."

Nera's eyes widen and she presses herself further into my side. "I'm happy to stay with my friends, but thank you." She smiles, but I can feel her hand tremble with nervousness.

I pat Shieran on his shoulder in a friendly manner. "Thank you for everything, General. Have a good night."

He clasps his hands behind his back and bows once more before walking back the way we came from the dining hall, leaving just the four of us in the dimly lit hallway. Nera leans her head against my shoulder, her eyes grateful as we all stand in silence.

True to his nature, Elex is the first to break the silence. "So, how are we splitting up tonight?"

Teyla quickly grabs Nera's free hand and tugs her away from me. "Easy. I say boys take one room, and us girls will take the other."

Uneasiness rises within me at that idea, and I shake my head. "I'm sorry, but I will not take my eyes off of Nera, even for a single night." I grasp her hand again. "Where she goes, I go."

Nera looks up at me with her eyebrows raised high. "And I have no say in this?" Her words say one thing, but I don't miss the way her fingers tighten around my hand.

I shake my head again. "You can try to keep me away, but I'm not going anywhere." I nod toward Teyla. "Your sister can even stay if she wants."

"Great," Elex grumbles. "So, it's just me all alone in a faerie mountain?"

"Aw, poor pup. How will you survive?" Teyla makes a pouty-face at Elex.

Nera touches Teyla's shoulder. "Come on, Tey. Just stay with him. We really should remain in pairs while here, and since I can't get rid of Reinor, you're stuck with Elex." A small smile graces her lips, and I try to hide my knowing grin. My mate is a little matchmaker.

Elex widens his eyes and sticks his lower lip out in a pout as he stares back at Teyla. Teyla groans, but she throws her hands up in defeat. "Fine. Just keep your hands to yourself, Pup. Got it?"

Elex scoffs and rolls his green eyes. "Not going to be a problem, Kitten."

The two of them continue to bicker as they enter the room on the left, shutting the door behind them. I sigh, letting my eyes fall on my mate whose shoulders slouch slightly now that we're alone.

"Come on," I say, dragging Nera into the second room with me.

Candles are already lit around the cozy bedroom, giving the carved stone walls an orange glow. I cross the room in just a few steps and take a seat on the bed, the smaller-sized mattress welcoming me with a sigh. It's a simple room with no decorations, but I'm grateful for it, knowing that Nera will need to remain close to me the whole night.

Nera moves toward me and sits at the other side of the bed, her head lowered as if she's deep in thought. I'm not having that.

I wrap my arms around her waist and drag her onto my lap. "Talk to me, Nera. What's on your mind?"

Her misty eyes flick up to mine and she smiles sadly. "Are you not capable of reading my mind...*mate*?"

That one word causes an exhilarating chill to roll up my spine and make me shiver. "That's dangerous, Nera."

Her eyebrows raise as she scans my face. "What's dangerous?"

"Calling me your *mate*. It's like you're claiming the title, and it does crazy things to my dragon." I lick my lips, already feeling my control wane.

Nera's lips curl up at the corners. "What if I want to claim it? To claim you..."

I close my eyes and take a deep breath. *Settle down*, I tell my dragon as his excitement rises. "You can't make that kind of decision yet," I whisper, locking eyes with Nera. "You've been hit with a lot of information tonight, so let's get some sleep, and we can talk about us another time."

She bites down softly on her bottom lip and nods. "Okay, but will you do something for me first?"

"Anything."

Her eyes shift to a heady dark turquoise color. "Kiss me, Reinor."

My hands instantly tighten around her waist. She doesn't need to tell me twice.

I lift Nera off of my lap and spin her onto the bed. She lands on her back, and I cover her small body with my warmth. I take a long look at her beneath me before I dip my head and allow our lips to connect.

The second our mouths meet, I'm consumed by fire. I explore her mouth with mine, tasting every inch of her lips. Her delicate fingers dance across my back, and then they slip into my hair, tugging gently at the strands.

Every touch just spurs me on, and I can't stop my own hands from exploring my mate. Our tongues tangle, and it's as if we have done this a million times before. How have I not been kissing this woman my entire life?

Nera makes a small moaning sound, and I can feel the scales of my dragon ripple across my skin. I pull back, keeping my eyes closed tight as I attempt to reign in the need to take everything that I can from her right here.

"Reinor?" Her voice makes me open my eyes. "Do you want to stop?"

I stroke her petal-soft cheek with my fingertips. "I really, *really* do not want to stop." I chuckle, causing a grin to light up her beautiful face. "But, I think it's best that we rest now."

She nods, but she doesn't move away from me as I turn onto my side. Instead, her head nuzzles beneath my chin and she tangles her arms and legs around my body. I hold her tight to my chest, feeling more at peace than I ever thought possible as we drift off to sleep.

CHAPTER 40

NERA

"What should I do, Dad?" I whisper into the empty room.

Dad? Yeah, that word sounds crazy coming from me. I had a dad once, my Pa in the Mortal Lands, but I never knew my birth father, the apparent late Fae king.

Trying to speak to the spirit of a man I never met just feels crazy, but I don't know what else to do. I'm lost. I need some sort of guidance.

Airden Faven, the current king of the Fae people, and my long lost cousin, has given me a choice to make. An impossible choice, in my opinion.

According to Airden, I can either embrace this ancient royal magic within me, and take my place on the Fae throne where I will lead a final war against the Blood Fae for the control of Faedom... *Or*, I can choose to rid myself of my responsibility by transferring my magic to my cousin, giving him the official role of king.

I don't know what entirely these options entail, but since meeting Airden just last night, this choice feels much too daunting. I need more time. I need fresh air. I need my family.

But I don't have a family anymore, do I? I have two dead Fae parents, a long lost human family a world away, and a cousin who I only just met. *Gods, I need help.*

I sigh loudly, throwing myself back on the bed I shared with Reinor all night. That is one thing that feels right, at least. Being held by Reinor for an entire night, feeling his heartbeat against my cheek and his breath in my hair. It was perfect. Of course, he *is* apparently my fated mate, which just makes things so much more complicated.

If I stay here in the Fae Wilds and become the Fae queen, Reinor has to leave me to return to his own kingdom. But if I give up my power and leave *with* him, I will never be accepted by his people.

I hear voices outside my bedroom door and sit up, wondering if any of my friends have returned. Teyla and Elex left this morning with General Shieran and his men to scout the woods surrounding the mountain.

Before she left to help the guards, Tey gave me her full support with whatever decision I make. Shortly after, Reinor went into the hall to keep watch over me, but wanted to give me time to think without him hovering. I'm about ready to make him come back in here before I drive myself crazy.

I stand up from the bed to go grab my mate, but a huffing sound behind me stops me in my tracks. I spin around, ready to scream, but I instead breathe out a long breath of relief.

"Smoke, you scared me!"

The massive Kitsune takes up half of the bedroom with her long, furry body. Her black hair swirls like smoke all over her, solidifying as she settles into the space from where she traveled through shadow to get here.

"How did you find me?" I reach out to touch her long snout, but pause when I see blood dripping from her mouth. "Smoke, are you hurt?"

Her head shakes from side to side and her large jaws open up to reveal a very bloody, and very dead bird the size of a turkey. She drops the bird at my feet before sitting back on her haunches with all nine of her fox tails wagging back and forth.

"Uhh..." I try not to let my nose scrunch up in disgust as I look down at the dead creature. I smile weakly at Smoke and gently pat her head which is higher than my own. "Thanks, Smoke. This is really...sweet of you."

She almost smiles as her black eyes stare down at me and she licks the extra blood from her lips. *Gross.*

I debate on whether to pick up the bird, or call Reinor in here to do my dirty work, when the bedroom door slowly opens behind me.

"Nera, can we tal—" Airden's voice stops when he fully enters the room and pauses at the sight of Smoke sitting beside me. His eyes widen and he crouches slightly as if readying to fight.

I hold my hands up. "This is Smoke, my Shadow Kitsune friend." I point down at the bloody bird at my feet. "I know she shouldn't be here without your permission, but she wanted to bring me a meal...I guess."

Airden nods slowly before standing back up straight, his alert blue wings relaxing behind him. "I'm assuming this animal has imprinted on you, then?"

"Yes, I saved her from a Dark Elf trap at the edge of the Wilds. Then she saved me shortly after when one of the Dark Elves tried to kill me." I smile back at Smoke.

Airden places his hands together and steps further into the room. "Well, it's good to meet you, uh...Smoke?" He clears his throat and focuses back on me. "Can we talk in private, or will Smoke be sticking around?"

I glance at Smoke who grumbles and narrows her eyes at Airden, and then I shrug my shoulders. "Looks like she's staying."

My cousin chuckles and shakes his head. "Alright, then. I'll only be a moment." His blue eyes—that I'm beginning to recognize as near perfect reflections of my own—soften as he looks down at me. "I know we didn't get a chance to go into detail last night, but I want you to fully understand your options."

I nod, feeling nervous as he continues. "I told you that you could keep the royal magic and take your place as queen, or you can give the magic over to me, but I didn't tell you what happens if you *do* relinquish your power." He looks at my pointed ears briefly. "There is no way to control the flow of power if we do the transfer ceremony, so you would be giving up all that you have, not just the royal magic. You would give up all that makes you Fae."

I pull my chin back, confused. "What do you mean by that?"

"It means that your ears would become rounded, you would lose the ability to grow wings, and your eyes would no longer change with your emotions." He sighs. "You would essentially become—"

"Human," I say, finishing his sentence.

Airden nods. "Yes, you would appear and act as a human." I bite on the inside of my lip as I consider his words. He must think this helps my decision, because he continues. "I want you to understand that I will not be upset when you take your rightful place as queen. I always hoped you'd return soon, even if this makes me take a step down."

I shake my head. "I haven't made the choice yet. You are still the king for the time being."

Airden tilts his head, confusion written across his face. "You would consider becoming a simple human?"

"Simple? I don't know what's so simple about being a human. I was raised by them, and those were the most wonderful years of my life."

He takes a moment to consider that as he watches me like I've grown two extra heads. "You're a unique person, Nera. I hope you know how lucky you are."

I scoff without meaning to. "Lucky? That's not a word I'd use to describe myself."

Airden smiles, but sadness still sits within his eyes. "Consider your life, Nera. I don't know a lot of what you've been through, but I know that you had a family for much of your life. You have friends in strange places, a powerful fated mate, and an entire kingdom ready to support you in whatever way you need. I'd call that pretty lucky, and maybe even well-deserved."

I'm struck dumb by his words, my mind racing with so many thoughts that I can't keep track of them, but Smoke brings me back to reality. She nudges the dead bird closer to me, and I freeze once the blood covers my bare foot.

Airden bends forward and lifts the bird by its broken wing, humor in his blue eyes. "Let me take this to the cook so he can prepare it for your dinner." He looks up at the glaring Kitsune. "Is that alright with you, Smoke?"

She hesitates but nods her head. Airden dips his head back at her, and then at me. "I'll leave you to your thoughts. Thanks for hearing me out, and please remember that I support you no matter what."

I wave goodbye to him as he leaves me and Smoke alone once more.

CHAPTER 41

REINOR

The evening sun is setting beyond the Fae Wilds, making this place look less wild and more calm as bugs flitter around, settling in for the night or just waking from their sleep.

I take a deep breath of the evergreen scent and imagine soaring above the treetops in my dragon form. I was informed that shifting here would only bring attention to the hiding Fae within the mountain, though.

"I can't believe you actually left Nera's side, man." Elex settles beside me on the boulder I found to rest upon.

After meeting Airden, Shieran, and the other Fae yesterday, I made sure to offer our services while we stayed in their home. Airden tried to brush it off, but I want to have a good relationship with the other kingdoms, unlike my father.

Teyla and Elex volunteered to help patrol the woods this morning, but I took Teyla's place this afternoon.

"Teyla is with her. She'll be safe with her sister and her people for a while." At least, I keep telling myself that. "This fated mate possessiveness is driving me insane. I'd like nothing more than to tie Nera to my back like a backpack so that she's never far from me."

Elex scoffs and shakes his head. He runs a hand through his blonde hair with a long groan of frustration. "I know exactly what you mean..."

My eyebrows shoot up to my hairline as I spin toward my best friend. "Wait, you *kind of* understand where I'm coming from, or you *know* know?"

His dark blue eyes flick up to mine and I know that same agony that I can see within him. "Turns out fate has chosen a damn *cat* as my mate, Reinor." He laughs and throws his head back with a wolfish growl. "Teyla would look great tied to my back, don't ya think?"

A loud laugh bursts from my lips as I smack Elex on his back. "Wow, congrats, man." I scan the woods ahead of us. "Are you happy about it?"

He sighs. "I'm so stupidly happy that I want to smack myself in my own face because I probably look like a lovesick puppy."

I turn and eye him. "You're right. You look like a total idiot." Elex punches me in the arm, making me curse in pain. "Didn't anyone ever teach you not to punch your king?"

Elex raises a single eyebrow my way. "You're lucky you only get a little tap from me, your highness." He glares, but I can see the humor written across his face.

I shake my head as I lean back on my hands, watching the sky slowly darken above us. "I've fought you before, and I don't plan on doing that again. It's incredibly humbling."

Elex chuckles, but the sound quickly fades, leaving just the noises of insects behind. After a pause, he leans on his elbows and looks my way. "I want to marry her, Reinor. I hope I can have your blessing. The blessing of our king."

I huff out an irritated breath. "You have my blessing in everything you do, Elex, but you don't need it. My father started that tradition, and I'm ending it. I have no interest in controlling the love lives of my people." I marvel at the happiness in my friend's eyes. "If you want her, and she wants you, don't hold back. Marry the *cat*." I grin, loving the fact that Elex is fated for a panther shifter.

He rolls his eyes and punches me much softer than before. "You're fated for a faerie. What exactly are you going to do about *that* situation, huh?"

I rub a hand along my face, too stressed to even think about it. "I have no idea, man. I love Nera so much, but she is stuck in between two worlds right now. I don't want to influence her decision in any way. It wouldn't be fair."

"Come on," he "tsks" at me with his tongue. "You don't have to tell her what to do, but you definitely need to let her know where you stand. Maybe she needs you to give her some guidance. She's probably terrified."

I nod. I know that she's scared, but the problem is that I'm scared too. I'm terrified of losing Nera when I only just got to be with her. "I think I need to go have a talk with my mate."

"You really, really do." He nods his head back toward the mountain. "When you get there, send *my* mate out to me. I have a question to ask her."

He winks, and it's my turn to smack him on the arm. "Quit rubbing in your easy happiness, you ass." I stand and hold my hand out for Elex to shake. "In all honesty, though. I'm happy for you."

He shakes my hand. "I'll be happy for you too when you finally pull your head out of the mud."

Classic Elex.

NERA

"Are you going to tell me why you seem extra perky this evening, Tey?" I eye my sister where she lays across the floor of mine and Reinor's bedroom with her black hair spread across Smoke's body.

Her head is resting against the Shadow Kitsune's side, as if Smoke was a giant pillow, and Smoke is snoring as she sleeps comfortably beneath Teyla. The two have really become close in such a short time.

Teyla avoids my piercing eyes and she bites onto her bottom lip. "I don't matter right now, Nera. Let's focus on you."

I roll my eyes with a groan. "Ugh, I'm so sick of talking about myself. I need you to pull me out of my head, if only for a few minutes."

"Fine." Tey sits up, and Smoke jolts awake only to settle right back down and continue snoring. "I have some news."

I lean forward at the edge of my bed, resting my hands on my knees. She is quiet for so long that I throw my hands up in the air. "Just tell me!"

Teyla smiles and her gray eyes practically sparkle against her warm tan skin. "Elex and I are fated mates." She says it so fast that I nearly miss it.

Once the words register in my head, I crawl off the bed and take my sister's hands in mine. "Are you serious, Tey? You and Elex?"

She nods, her smile growing by the second. "Yes, and I love him already so much that I want to scream! Even though he irritates the hell out of me."

I laugh along with her, and tears brim my eyes. "Oh, wow, Tey. That is so amazing, and I'm so happy for you." I squeeze her hand. "Thank the gods that you didn't marry Mathis Longborn!"

She laughs loudly and throws her head back. "Oh, thank you, thank you, thank you!" She shouts to the ceiling.

"This is incredible," I say. "Elex is such a good man, and if anyone could deserve you, it might just be him. Does he love you with that passion you always dreamt of?"

The kind of passion I have with Reinor.

Teyla nods. "I really never thought I could have this in my life, but thanks to you, I can have real happiness."

My eyebrows press together. "Thanks to me?"

"Duh," she says matter-of-factly. "Even though I tried to warn you away from those forbidden woods, you kept going to see Reinor every month. You led me to Reinor, which led me to Elex. Without you, I'd be married to a boring, lifeless man who still lives with his parents."

I shake my head. "I'm so glad you found your destiny." My hand travels to the dragon pendant around my neck, and I hold it tight. If only I could find my own destiny.

Teyla's eyes follow the movement of my hand, and her hand covers mine. "I always wondered why you connected with this golden dragon pendant so much. It makes perfect sense now, though. The golden dragon is Reinor, and he is your destiny."

I look down at the golden gem at the center of the dragon's eye. "You think the gem worked? That it brought me to Reinor?"

"The jeweler woman said it herself the day we went into that shop. The necklace was enchanted by the Fae, *your people*, and it was meant to guide you on your perfect path. Even that Madame Karista woman said it last night. You had to go through everything in order to realize your fated mate bond with Reinor, and then to find out where you truly came from. Why not just bring you here when you were twelve and make you the Fae queen? Why was meeting your mate so important?" She grabs the pendant and places it beside my heart. "Because Reinor is your destiny, Nera."

I blink a few times in the silence, trying to keep my tears at bay. If Reinor and I are meant to be forever, then I have to turn my back on my father's kingdom, his legacy.

The silence in the room is broken as the bedroom door opens and Smoke jumps to her four massive paws in a protective stance.

Reinor peeks around the Kitsune and his golden eyes land on me. "Hey, can we talk?"

CHAPTER 42

NERA

"Of course." I scramble to my feet, and Teyla follows me.

"I'll go find Elex," Teyla says, laying her hand on Smoke's neck. "Wanna come for a walk with me, big girl? We can scare a bunch of faeries in the halls."

Smoke turns her head toward me as if to ask if I'm okay with her leaving. I stroke the black hair on her back and nod. "Go ahead. I'll be here the whole time."

Teyla and Smoke walk around Reinor, and Smoke has to duck to fit her body through the open door. Once they're gone, Reinor closes the door and the room is suddenly filled with an uncomfortable silence.

"So," I say, twirling my fingers together. "You wanted to talk?"

"Yes." Reinor begins pacing around the room, his golden eyes flicking toward me off and on. His boots make a hollow thud against the stone floor.

My nerves are running wild, so I reach out and place my hands against Reinor's chest, stopping his movements. "Is everything okay? You're kind of scaring me."

Reinor's eyes connect with mine, and a smile stretches his lips. *Gods, he's gorgeous.* His face has grown a little more hair since we left on this journey, and his brown hair is nearly touching his eyebrows at this point.

His large hands move to the sides of my face, and he quickly pulls me close to him, connecting our lips before I know what's happening. An electric jolt courses through my body that makes me take a quick breath.

The kiss is over much too soon as Reinor lifts his head and meets my gaze again. "Everything is perfect as long as I have you in my arms, Nera." I can't help but smile at his words and I lean in to kiss him again, but he stops me with his thumb stroking along my lips. "But I need you to hear me out for a moment."

"Okay…" I stand straighter and take a much needed step back, but Reinor doesn't release me.

His hands slide down my neck, across my shoulders, and down my arms, leaving a trail of tingles until he links his fingers with mine. "I know we haven't talked much today. I've been trying to give you space to think clearly, but I heard what Airden told you earlier. I know what the consequences of your choices will be, and I want you to know where I stand." He chuckles softly. "If you even care about my thoughts on the matter of your future."

I'm sure my face shows how ridiculous I find that thought. "Of course I care about what you think. You're my mate, Reinor."

Reinor's hands tighten on mine, and his golden-brown eyes light up and begin to glow, but he shakes his head to get rid of the bright gold. "As you can see, just hearing you call me yours is enough to fill me with so much hope." He takes a deep breath. "I love you, Nera. I know you already know that, but it needs to be said as often as I possibly can say it. I love you with all that I am, and I would have loved you forever, even if I was never told that fate chose us for one another. I believed you were my destiny before that woman said anything."

My heart flutters in my chest. I can feel the truth in his words, and all I want to do is say the same thing back to him, but he continues talking.

"Here's what I can give you. Take what option you wish, but do it for yourself, and *your* happiness. I will never be happy if you aren't happy anyways." He licks his lips and strokes his thumbs along the backs of my hands. "Option one...If you choose to claim the Fae throne as yours, and keep the royal magic, you will need to stay in Faedom. I will fight by your side to take back the kingdom, and watch you rise to be the greatest queen that this land has ever seen. But, I will return back to the shifters and make my home better than it ever was before. I have plans for the City of Shifters, and I owe it to my people to see those plans through."

I swallow a thick lump in my throat, and my heart threatens to crack. "And option two?" My voice wobbles on the question.

His eyes pierce into mine as if he can see through them. "Option number two is that you give up your magic, and all that makes you Fae. This doesn't mean you'd be giving up who you truly are, just parts of you that need to remain in this land. In that case, you could return home with me, Nera." He drops to his knees before me, stopping my heart completely. "You wouldn't look like a faerie anymore, which means you'd never have to hide. The shifters would accept my human mate as their queen. You would be *my* queen, my *equal* for the rest of our lives and far beyond. *My Nera.*"

I blink back the tears that want to fall as I drop to my knees with Reinor. "You want me forever, Reinor? Are you sure about that?"

His eyebrows shoot up as he smiles wide. "It's not my choice, but yes. I will support you and worship you for as long as I'm allowed. Whether that be near or far."

I wipe at my eyes with the back of my hand. "I don't know what to say."

He shrugs. "If you need a third option, you could always choose to say 'get lost, Reinor,' and you'll never have to see my dragon ass again." I laugh loudly and the grin he gives me is enough to light this whole room on fire.

I shake my head. "I don't like that option, but I don't know if I'm ready to pick one of the others either."

"Then don't pick yet. Think about it."

"Can I kiss you while I think?" I ask as I snake my arms around his neck.

Reinor growls like an animal before crashing his lips to mine, once again taking my breath away. I guess that's a *yes.*

CHAPTER 43

NERA

It's well into the night now, and the large gathering room within the mountain is becoming more empty by the minute. I sit with Reinor, Teyla, Elex, and some of the guards that just came in for a late dinner after their patrols.

Elex is in celebration after asking Teyla to marry him. She said yes, of course, and one of the Fae guards has challenged Elex to a drinking game.

I've never had Fae wine—or any wine for that matter—but it seems to affect shifters less than it does the Fae. Tey is laughing with the biggest grin on her beautiful face as her fiancé shouts his love for her to the cavern ceiling and downs his fifth glass while his opponent groans and gives up.

The few stragglers all cheer when Elex takes Teyla by the waist and kisses her deeply for all to see. I laugh at the show, and cheer extra loud for my sister and friend.

A faerie woman comes around and clears the plates in front of me that once held a deliciously cooked bird thanks to Smoke's disgusting offering. Without all of the mangled feathers and blood, the bird made a great meal. I'll need to be sure to thank Smoke when she chooses to appear again.

A door off to the back of the cavern opens and in walks Airden. His eyes scan the room until they find me and he walks over to our little group.

"I'm glad you're still up, Nera. I've thought about this a lot, and I think you need to see something." He pulls out a folded up piece of paper and places it in my hand.

I look down at the paper, confused. "What is this?"

His eyes shift to a sad gray color. "It's a letter from my uncle…your father." He holds his hands up before I can freak out. "I know I should have given it to you sooner, but I wanted you to make a decision of your own, without feeling like I'm trying to push you one way or the other."

I stare at the paper, and my hands begin to tremble. "How did you get this? I thought my father was killed."

"He was, but the night that his soldiers found his body, he was holding this letter in his hands. He wrote it to my handlers, so that they could find you in case something happened to him. After discovering the letter, they looked for you, but you were gone already." Airden looks at my friends who have now grown silent, and then his blue eyes find mine again. "I don't believe I'm capable of loving someone. It's not in the cards for me, but your father clearly believed in love like no one else." He dips his head. "I'll leave you to it."

Airden walks back out of the room, leaving me frozen in place with my father's last words sitting between my fingers.

Reinor leans in and touches my cheek softly, drawing my attention to him. "Read it, Nera. We will give you some privacy."

He presses his lips to my forehead and then everyone in the room scatters. Reinor, Elex, and Teyla stand beside the cavern's opening, facing away from me but staying close.

I take a steadying breath and open the paper, where words are sprawled out in black ink, written fast and sloppy.

To the brave Fae of the mountain,
If you are reading this enchanted writing, you must have a good heart. I don't have much time. My daughter is alive, and she is the future queen of Faedom. She is beautiful, just like her mother. She and I are being hunted by at least three of the Blood Fae that killed my wife. I have no choice but to leave my princess and lead these monsters away from her.

By some miracle, I will live and this letter will be unnecessary, but in the case of my death, which I fear is likely to come shortly, take care of my baby girl.

She rests beyond the borders of our world, in the Night Woods beside the Mortal Lands. Follow the magic, and you will find my enchantment that I placed to protect her from harm.

Please bring her home. This war will end with the next generation, but our people need the royal magic if we are to survive. -Your king

Now for my daughter,
I hope that you will never have to read this letter, for this must mean that I am gone. But, if you must grow up without me in your life, know these two things.

First, you do not need to be what the Fae expect you to be. Your mother was a simple woman from a simple family, and she never wanted you to live the life of a royal. The pressure that I grew up with is heavy, and if I were there, I would let you choose your path like I never could.

Second, put love first. Whether it be the love of your kingdom, as a queen, or the love of your family, as a daughter, sister, cousin, and someday mother. Or whether it be the love of your chosen mate. Love isn't taught to our kind the way it should be, so always remember to hold onto it. It's the best thing we have.

I love you, my angel. You have already proven your strength in just your first day of life, so always keep that strength with you.
Until we meet again.

My hands tremble as I lay the paper on the table in front of me. Reinor is at my side in an instant, his palms cradling my face. "Nera, why are you crying?"

I blink and realize that he's right. Tears are streaming from my eyes and down my cheeks. "He loved me. My father loved me and he gave me the answers that I needed without even knowing I would need them." I scoff and shake my head. "Destiny is one real piece of work, you know that?"

I look into Reinor's worried eyes as he brushes my tears away with his thumbs. "You've lost me, my love. What did the letter say? Are you going to be alright?"

I sniffle and nod, smiling over his shoulder at Elex and Teyla, then back at Reinor. They are the family I have had all along without even realizing it. They are my home, and for some reason it took me this long to realize that all I want is them.

"I know what I want, Reinor." I can feel his body tense before me as he holds his breath. "I choose you. A life with you, bettering *our* kingdom and growing together…forever."

I can hear Teyla gasp, but my focus is on my mate as his eyes brim with tears and his forehead falls gently against mine. "I love you so much, Nera."

"I love you too, Reinor"

CHAPTER 44

NERA

Music floats around the large gathering room, echoing off of the high ceilings and filtering out into the many halls within this mighty mountain.

This is Fae-song, an enchanted melody that cannot be recreated with any ordinary instrument. It's the most lovely sound I've ever heard, and I'm grateful I got to hear it before I leave.

More Fae than I have ever seen in one place surround me where I stand at the center-most part of the cavern. Their eyes all shimmer with a new hope as I prepare to give my magic for their future.

And it feels right.

"Are you ready, Nera?" Airden is standing before me, Shieran to his left, and Madame Karista to his right.

I nod and let my cousin take my hands in his much larger ones. "You deserve this magic, Airden. I believe you will do incredible things for Faedom."

Airden's face shows little emotion, but I can see the strong tick of his jaw as he tries to remain the stoic king he was raised to be. He dips his head to me and then closes his eyes.

As planned, Madame Karista moves to my side and begins to whisper instruction to me, guiding me through this process.

I glance to my right where Reinor, Teyla, and Elex stand with the anxious Fae crowd. I take one last long look at my made-family, praying to the gods that they will look the same to me with new human eyes.

Madame Karista clears her throat. "Close your eyes, dear." I follow her instructions. "Now, imagine sinking within yourself, toward that power that has been inside of you your entire life. It has a solid form that only you can see." I know exactly what she's talking about, and I find the magic instantly. It's a bright orb of energy that the Elf woman, Lanya, taught me to locate. "You can release that power by pulling at it piece by piece until it spreads through all parts of your body."

I nod, doing as she says. The magic flows within me, warming my insides and making me feel like a ball of heat that can just float away.

Airden's voice breaks into my mind. "I can feel the magic, Nera. It's strong."

"It's too strong," I say. I've never liked the feeling of this immense power that is wild and uncontrollable. Hopefully Airden can control better than I could.

"Now," Karista continues. "The magic is spread thin enough for you to start to bleed it out through your fingertips, and into Airden." I imagine it exactly as she says, like blood leaving an open wound where Airden and I connect. "Repeat after me, Nera."

Karista begins to talk and I repeat her words. "This transfer of magic is freely given, from my spirit to yours. The power of my ancestors, through blood, and through time, will belong to you until the first born of your brood, and on thereafter."

An enormous weight that I hadn't felt until this very moment is lifted from my person. I gasp, feeling featherlight and completely new, reborn. It's a feeling of stress relief, only one thousand fold. It's...amazing.

"Open your eyes, Nera."

I blink as Airden releases my hands. I don't know what I expected, but my cousin is looking back at me, confused, but otherwise unchanged.

"Did it work?" I ask, looking around at the crowd who are staring back at me in awe.

I turn toward Karista and she smiles kindly. "You are every bit as beautiful as you were before, but the magic is gone from you."

I nod, reaching up and tentatively touching my ears. The tips are round where they were once pointed, making me squeal at the crazy feeling. The entire crowd of Fae begin to laugh as they watch my reaction, and then they erupt in cheers.

The room becomes chaotic as voices mix together and chatter fills the cave. Many people disperse back through the tunnels, being guided by General Shieran and his soldiers.

"Thank you, cousin," Airden says, bringing my attention back to him. "Even though you are no longer technically a faerie, you will always be my family."

I smile back at him. "Do you feel...different? Like, more powerful?"

He holds his hands out and studies them, flipping them around. "I feel pretty much the same, but I suppose it will take time for me to learn to access the magic as you had." He sighs, and then he quickly pulls me into a very stiff hug. "You have given my people hope once more, and I will never be able to repay you for that."

I pull back and look up into his bright purple eyes. "Just win, okay? That's all I want."

"I will."

"And we will help you." Reinor's voice sounds behind me.

I spin around to face my mate, suddenly worried that he won't like the new me as much as the Fae version. "We're going to help them fight?"

His golden-brown eyes smile down at me. "Yes, we must. Our kingdoms are joined by family now."

"No," Airden says, surprising me. "You will not fight the Blood Fae with us."

Reinor crosses his arms. "Why not? We can return home and gather the shifter army. We can march on your capital in just a few weeks."

Before I can open my mouth to agree with Reinor, Airden speaks again. "As much as I appreciate your offer of assistance, this is not your fight, King Reinor." Reinor tries to argue, but Airden holds a hand up. "I plan to harness this new power and strike the Blood Fae in just one week. You won't make it back in time, and even if you could, I wouldn't want you to risk your army only weeks after becoming king. Your people will never trust you after such a move."

"And the Fae will be okay with you starting a war a week after getting the royal magic?" I ask, worried for him.

Airden shakes his head. "The Blood Fae started this war years ago. The people of Faedom are more than ready to end it."

Reinor is silent as his arm wraps around my waist. "You're certain of this, Airden?"

He nods, an air of confidence around him. "I am more than certain…it's time."

CHAPTER 45

REINOR

"I never thought it would feel this good to be home." Teyla stands at the base of the canyon, her eyes on the morning horizon where the City of Shifters rests.

Elex drags her into his arms and kisses her cheek. "It's because you're going to be living with me, isn't it, Kitten?"

Her gray panther eyes narrow on her mate. "Call me *Kitten* again, and I'll be moving into the castle with my sister...*permanently.*"

"Oh, please," Elex scoffs. "You'd miss me way too much." His nose nuzzles her neck, causing her to giggle and shove at him.

"You wish," she says, causing Elex to growl and begin chasing her across the field of grass between us and the towering stone castle ahead.

"Gosh, they are just too cute." Nera sighs, and I let my gaze fall on her.

Her wavy brown hair is loose around her newly round ears, brushing against the splash of freckles across her shoulders. The cold wind picks up and breathes goosebumps along her arms, causing her to shiver and rub her hands over her skin for warmth.

"Ugh, why does being practically human mean I have to be even colder than before?" Her eyes flick up to meet mine and she pauses. "Why are you staring at me, your highness?"

A smile tugs at my lips, and I temporarily get lost in her golden-brown eyes. Eyes that mirror my own. "You are breathtaking. I could stare at you day in and day out for the rest of my life."

A pink blush stains her cheeks as she slowly begins to saunter my way. "It's the new eye color, isn't it? You must really like yourself if you love me even more now that I just *happen* to have similar eyes to yours." Her finger pokes my chest. "Cocky, cocky king."

I snatch her hand out of the air between us and pull her body against mine, the rest of the world temporarily forgotten. "I love you more every single time you look in my direction, my Nera. Seeing a piece of me in your eyes is merely a happy bonus."

She grins back at me, her tongue peeking out to slide along her bottom lip. "You are a smooth talker, Reinor."

"Only for you." I lean down, aching to take my time kissing those lips, but something large and black breaks us apart.

"Smoke!" Nera shouts, laughing as the shadow beast swipes her massive tongue along my mate's face. "Gross!"

I reach out and save Nera from the wet torture. "Go back to the shadows, Smoke. You've had enough of her time over the past three days."

Especially since Smoke insists on sleeping beside Nera in every place we make camp. I know she's just being protective of Nera because of how they first met out in the woods, but I'm ready for some alone time already. *With Nera, not the Kitsune.*

Smoke growls and glares back at me, but she doesn't shove her way back in between us. Instead, she turns and runs in the direction that Elex and Teyla left.

"I don't understand why she is still following me around," Nera says beside me. "I'm not powerful anymore. I don't even have pointed ears or colorful wings."

I shake my head. "Are you upset that you will never have wings? Do you regret giving them up?"

Nera smiles up at me, snaking her small arms around my neck. "Absolutely not. I have a family now, and a gorgeous, golden dragon mate with the best wings in the world." One of her eyebrows raises as she grins. "I'll just make you fly me around whenever I want."

I laugh as an idea pops into my head. "Your wish is my command, my love."

I take a step away from Nera and call my dragon forward. It has been too long since I shifted last, so he is ready and excited. I'm fully shifted within seconds, and my large wings stretch wide to either side of me. I lower my head to the ground beside Nera, hoping that she's not scared.

She surprises me by giggling and easily sliding onto my scaled back. Exhilaration floods me at the idea of carrying my mate through the sky, so I launch into the air, loving the excited squeal that leaves her lips.

We fly easily over the wide field, and over the castle grounds. I spot Elex, Teyla, and Smoke who all walk up the castle steps, their heads tilted back as they watch me soar past them. It's early morning, so the courtyard is still empty, aside from one face that I've never seen before, but I know who it is instantly.

A new hope spurs me forward, so I quickly drop in elevation while Nera hangs on tight. I land heavy on the stones of the castle courtyard, and I let Nera climb back off of my neck.

"Wow, that was incredible, Reinor!" She leans toward me and kisses what could be considered my dragon's cheek. She looks around at the nearly empty courtyard and I know the very moment she sees the only other person out here with us.

I call my dragon forward, shifting just in time to catch Nera in my arms as she collapses with a sharp intake of air, her voice a rasp as she speaks. "Ma?"

CHAPTER 46

NERA

I'm dreaming. I have to be dreaming, don't I?

Standing just a few yards in front of me, her brown eyes exactly as I remember them, though new wrinkles line her beautiful face, is my mother. *My human mother.*

My body shakes uncontrollably, my mind fearing that I must be dreaming, and I can feel myself begin to fall as my legs give out. I don't hit the ground, though as Reinor catches me in his bare arms.

"Ma?" I ask, temporarily not caring that my sexy mate is currently in nothing but a pair of black pants.

My mother's eyes fill with tears as she charges toward me. "My baby girl!"

Before I even tell my legs to move, I'm running and crashing into my Ma's distantly familiar arms. She holds me so tight that I can hardly breathe, but I don't care even a little bit. I'm only barely aware that I'm sobbing into her graying brown hair that smells like a home I nearly forgot ever existed.

"Ma, how are you—"

"Nera Deera!" A voice cuts me off, and I freeze in my mother's arms.

This isn't possible.

Ma releases me only to open her arms and let another person into our embrace. It's my brother.

"Benjamin," I whisper, unable to find my full voice.

My brother lifts me and my mother both off the ground in a huge bear hug. He pulls his head back and I'm struck dumb at the man standing before me.

He's tall and insanely muscular. A behemoth of a man with a full manly beard. The only thing that hasn't changed is his kind eyes that look at me with the brotherly love I thought I lost years ago.

"How are you guys here?" My words come out shaky and strange as I try to stop my sobs. "Am I dreaming? Please tell me this is real."

Ma's gentle hands cup my cheeks as her tear-filled eyes connect with mine. "This is real, my girl. It's a dream come true."

"A crazy, supernatural dream come true," Benjamin adds, shocking me with the deep tone of his voice.

I blink rapidly as I look from Ma to Ben and back again. One question fills my mind. "Is Pa—" I can't finish the sentence.

Benjamin lays a hand on my shoulder and shakes his head with sadness in his dark eyes. "Pa was badly injured that...the night you left." He swallows hard. "He didn't make it to morning."

I nod, understanding. Sadness and happiness become a crazy mix within my heart, and I have so many questions that I can't possibly begin to pick one. A moment later, I feel warmth against my back that soothes me.

I turn to find Reinor standing behind me with worry in his eyes. "Reinor, this is—" I struggle to find a way to explain these people that I thought I would never see again. "This is my family." I take his hand in mine. "Ma, Ben, this is King Reinor Iredras. He's my fated mate."

Ma lets out a loud, sniffling sob. "Calder didn't tell us you were fated mates. Oh, Nera." She wraps me in her arms once more, pulling Reinor into a hug as well. "I'm so happy that you found true love after everything."

I wipe at my eyes, a happy smile on my face. "I did, Ma. Just like you said I would." Then a thought occurs to me. "Wait, did you say Calder? How do you know Calder? And how are you guys even here in the City of Shifters and at the castle?"

Before they can answer, Calder himself steps out of the castle doors with a cocky grin on his handsome face. "Welcome home bro," he says to Reinor with his hands in the air. "Can you believe I found them? Am I good or what?"

I spin toward Reinor with my eyes so wide that they hurt. "Did you do this, Reinor? What is he talking about?"

Calder scoffs. "Excuse me, but *I* am the one who found the long lost humans. Reinor was just the idea man."

I look between Calder and Reinor, losing my patience fast. "When? Why? How?"

Reinor, Ma, and Benjamin all chuckle, rocking my world with the sound, but it's Reinor who finally speaks. "Before we left the city, I asked Calder to take a few men and return to the Night Woods where I found you all those years ago. I asked him to attempt to locate your family and invite them back here." He gently strokes my cheeks. "So you could have your family again."

"Gods." A new round of tears begin to flow. "How did you even know where to look?"

Calder laughs, making us all look back at him. "All he gave me was a last name and a location in the middle of the woods. It's a damn good thing dragons have the best sense of smell and tracking than any other creature. And it's lucky your family never moved to a different location. Your scent was still on their property after years."

I whip my head toward Benjamin and Ma. Ben winks at me. "Ma and I stayed put in the hopes that you'd find your way back home someday. I never expected a dragon shifter prince to come knocking, though."

Ma touches Calder's arm, making him suddenly look like a boy and less like the full-of-himself man. "He was very sweet and flew us both on his dragon's back all the way here. We left everything behind and never looked back."

The courtyard grows silent as we all just stare at one another, my heart so full it could burst.

Benjamin is the one to break the silence. "Eh, the humans were always too dull for me anyways. I'm ready to meet some hot shifter women." He wiggles his eyebrows and we all burst into laughter.

CHAPTER 47

NERA

How could I possibly sleep with my mother snoring softly just a few feet away?

I stare in awe, feeling incredibly creepy as I watch her shoulders rise and fall with her breaths where she sleeps in my bed. I'm back in my old bedroom in the castle, across the hall from Reinor.

I wanted nothing more than to spend the night in his bed now that we are back "home", but I have spent the entire day with Ma and Benjamin, catching up and getting to know them all over again. I have been afraid to leave Ma's side and wake up from this unbelievable dream.

I don't know what exactly my future looks like here in this castle with Reinor as king, but I have real hope. And the fact that I have my family here with me is enough to make every one of my wishes come true. If only Pa were here too, then all of the pieces would be exactly where they belong.

I jump as a knock on my door breaks me from my thoughts, and I hurry over to answer before another knock can wake Ma.

I swing the door open quietly to find my smiling brother on the other side. "Ben, what's up? I thought you went to bed."

He shakes his head. "Nah, I had a little talk with your fated mate instead." He raises an eyebrow before grinning. "Big brother approves."

I roll my eyes, feeling like a kid again. "And you have a say in who I choose to love, huh?"

Ben leans against my door frame with his large arms crossed. "Hey, a few years away doesn't unmake a family, Nera Deera. You will always be my baby sister."

I s]]have to bite my tongue to keep the dang tears at bay. "You are absolutely right about that."

He tugs me into his arms and hugs me tightly before spinning me around and shoving me out of my bedroom in my nightgown. "I'll stay with Ma. I think *your* room is across the hall." He winks before chuckling and shutting the door in my face.

My jaw drops and I look around in confusion. I guess I'll get to spend the night with my mate after all.

I turn and gently knock on Reinor's bedroom door. It's only a few seconds before the door swings open and I'm pulled into the arms of the love of my life. My destiny.

Reinor shuts the door behind me with his foot and then his lips are on mine. Every part of my body melts into him as he explores my mouth with his.

I reach out and wrap my arms around his neck, deepening the kiss and pressing as close to him as I can, desperate for just a little more.

Reinor groans against me, his hands stroking my sides, my arms, my neck, never stopping.

"I am yours," he whispers between kisses. "Forever." His lips leave mine after a long taste and then he drops his forehead against mine. "Marry me, Nera."

I'm breathless, but my mind is alert enough to hear his plea. "Just like that? You weaken my resolve and then ask me to marry you while I'm a puddle at your feet?"

He bends and drops to one knee. "I'm at *your* feet, my love." He smiles, and the look on his face has me sighing. "You are everything to me, Nera. I felt the tug fate had on me the very moment I saw you when we were mere children. I knew I could never be without you for as long as I live, and I will do whatever it takes to give you the life you deserve. A happy, fulfilled, and love-filled existence. You will be my queen, loved by my people." His hands take hold of mine as he stares up at me from the floor. "Marry me, Nera."

I bite down on my bottom lip and nod. "You know I will, Reinor. I'm yours just as you are mine."

He bursts up from the ground and takes me in his arms, lifting me off my feet. I let out a joyous giggle and wrap my arms around his neck.

Reinor plops me on my back on top of his bed with an animal-like growl as his mouth claims mine all over again. He runs his hands over my body, as if he needs to touch every inch of me.

His lips leave mine to trail kisses across my jaw and down my neck. He tastes the base of my neck and I shiver with a sudden heat that I have never felt before this moment.

My breath hitches and I feel him smile against my skin before his lips crash back down on mine again. He raises his head, his hands gripping my hips as he lowers his body against mine.

His golden eyes shine brightly above me. "Will you stay with me tonight, my Nera? And every night after this one?"

I wrap my legs around his waist and tug him closer to me before whispering against his lips. "For my entire life, and far, far beyond."

**Thank you for reading A Fae's Fate!
I truly loved writing these characters and their adventure! But I'm not done with this world yet...
Coming soon: King Airden Faven's story of learning to trust, opening his heart, and taking back his kingdom once and for all!**

Until then, have you read any of my other books? Check these completed series out below, all available on Kindle Unlimited:

The Intended Series

The Rescued Series

Hidden Cure Series

The Kingdom Trials Series

Destiny Born Series

The Wolf Hunted Series

Wolfe Asylum Series

REVIEW THIS BOOK

It means so much to me that you bought my book! Writing is such a passion of mine and I look forward to your feedback.

So, if you liked this book, whether it be the characters, settings, or adventures, I'd like to ask you a small favor. Hop on over to Amazon and leave a review with your thoughts. It'd be so great to read what YOU have to say!

From your friend, Abigail Grant

OTHER BOOKS BY ABIGAIL

Exclusive Freebies:

A Vision in Thessaly: The Intended Series Prequel

Shifter Cure: Hidden Cure Series Prequel

A Trial of Vengeance: The Kingdom Trials Prequel

Ash Born: Destiny Born Series Prequel

Amazon Series Pages:

The Intended Series

The Rescued Series

Hidden Cure Series

The Kingdom Trials Series

Destiny Born Series

The Wolf Hunted Series

Wolfe Asylum Series

A Fae's Fate Series

Printed in Great Britain
by Amazon